ISBN 978-0-282-50836-4
PIBN 10854196

1 MONTH OF
FREE
READING

at

www.ForgottenBooks.com

By purchasing this book you are eligible for one month membership to ForgottenBooks.com, giving you unlimited access to our entire collection of over 1,000,000 titles via our web site and mobile apps.

To claim your free month visit:
www.forgottenbooks.com/free854196

English
Français
Deutsche
Italiano
Español
Português

www.forgottenbooks.com

Mythology Photography **Fiction**
Fishing Christianity **Art** Cooking
Essays Buddhism Freemasonry
Medicine **Biology** Music **Ancient
Egypt** Evolution Carpentry Physics
Dance Geology **Mathematics** Fitness
Shakespeare **Folklore** Yoga Marketing
Confidence Immortality Biographies
Poetry **Psychology** Witchcraft
Electronics Chemistry History **Law**
Accounting **Philosophy** Anthropology
Alchemy Drama Quantum Mechanics
Atheism Sexual Health **Ancient History**
Entrepreneurship Languages Sport
Paleontology Needlework Islam
Metaphysics Investment Archaeology
Parenting Statistics Criminology
Motivational

icroreproductions / Institut canadien de microreproductions historiques

1998

The Institute has attempted to obtain the best
original copy available for filming. Features of this
copy which may be bibliographically unique,
which may alter any of the images in the
reproduction, or which may significantly change
the usual method of filming, are checked below.

L'In
qu'il
de c
poir
une
moc
son1

☑ Coloured covers/
Couverture de couleur

☐

☑ Covers damaged/
Couverture endommagée

☑

☐ Covers restored and/or laminated/
Couverture restaurée et/ou pelliculée

☐

☐ Cover title missing/
Le titre de couverture manque

☑

☐ Coloured maps/
Cartes géographiques en couleur

☐

☐ Coloured ink (i.e. other than blue or black)/
Encre de couleur (i.e. autre que bleue ou noire)

☐

☑ Coloured plates and/or illustrations/
Planches et/ou illustrations en couleur

☐

☐ Bound with other material/
Relié avec d'autres documents

☐

☐ Tight binding may cause shadows or distortion
along interior margin/
La reliure serrée peut causer de l'ombre ou de la
distorsion le long de la marge intérieure

☐

☐

☐ Blank leaves added during restoration may
appear within the text. Whenever possible, these
have been omitted from filming/
Il se peut que certaines pages blanches ajoutées
lors d'une restauration apparaissent dans le texte,
mais, lorsque cela était possible, ces pages n'ont

L'exemplaire filmé fut reproduit grâce à la générosité de:

Les images suivantes ont été reproduites avec le plus grand soin, compte tenu de la condition et de la netteté de l'exemplaire filmé, et en conformité avec les conditions du contrat de filmage.

Les exemplaires originaux dont la couverture en papier est imprimée sont filmés en commençant par le premier plat et en terminant soit par la dernière page qui comporte une empreinte d'impression ou d'illustration, soit par le second plat, selon le cas. Tous les autres exemplaires originaux sont filmés en commençant par la première page qui comporte une empreinte d'impression ou d'illustration et en terminant par la dernière page qui comporte une telle empreinte.

Un des symboles suivants apparaîtra sur la dernière image de chaque microfiche, selon le cas: le symbole ➔ signifie "A SUIVRE", le symbole ▽ signifie "FIN".

Les cartes, planches, tableaux, etc., peuvent être filmés à des taux de réduction différents. Lorsque le document est trop grand pour être reproduit en un seul cliché, il est filmé à partir de l'angle supérieur gauche, de gauche à droite, et de haut en bas, en prenant le nombre d'images nécessaire. Les diagrammes suivants illustrent la méthode.

1

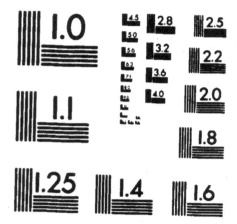

MICROCOPY RESOLUTION TEST CHART
NATIONAL BUREAU OF STANDARDS
STANDARD REFERENCE MATERIAL 1010a
(ANSI and ISO TEST CHART No. 2)

" Nansen tore down to the water's edge, and plunged into the icy sea."

A. 268.

'MID SNOW AND ICE.

Stories of Peril in Polar Seas.

CHARLES D. MICHAEL,

Author of "Heroes All," "Through Flame and Flood," etc.

" To reside
In thrilling regions of thick-ribbed ice
To be imprisoned in the viewless winds
And blown with restless violence round about
The pendent world."—*Shakespeare.*

TORONTO :
THE MUSSON BOOK COMPANY,
LIMITED.

PREFACE.

"THE only great thing left undone in the world" So the conquest of the Arctic regions was described by Sir Martin Frobisher when, in 1576, he set sail in his three cockle shells, valiantly determined that the "great thing" should at last be accomplished.

But it has taken all the bravery of hundreds of brave men through nearly three-and-a-half centuries of time to achieve even the partial conquest of those grim solitudes of perpetual snow and ice, amid whose fastnesses the secrets of the polar regions have been so jealously kept.

For even now, although the actual race to the north and south extremities of the world is over, much remains for science to do in those vast icy wastes that lie within the Arctic and Antarctic circles; and there is room yet for the exercise of heroism as great as that which has been shown in the efforts of men towards the supreme tasks which have at last been accomplished.

Lavish indeed has been the expenditure of life and treasure upon polar problems, and many and varied have been the motives which have prompted it.

Originally it was the hope of finding an open north-western or north-eastern route to the Orient. There was also the prospect of exploiting the great m'neral wealth which was supposed by some sanguine adventurers to be hidden beneath the eternal snows of the far north. But to-day, when the fascination of exploration and discovery is as strong in the hearts of men as ever it was, the reason that urges Arctic and Antarctic voyagers to deeds of bravery is not the prospect of discovering any new trade route amid the far northern icy seas, nor the hope of finding wealth beneath farthest southern snows. It is solely that certain scientific problems ; ay once and for all be solved.

The motive is indeed a high one, and the end to be attained may even yet demand immense sacrifices. True it is that the honour of being first at the north and south poles has not fallen to the lot of Englishmen; but at least we have the satisfaction of knowing that it was the work of British explorers that made success for others possible. And we know, too, that the men of our race are ready to meet whatever further demands upon courage and endurance may be necessary to complete the work of exploration in the northern and southern extremities of the world.

CONTENTS.

LIST OF ILLUSTRATIONS.

'MID SNOW AND ICE.

CHAPTER I.

MAN'S FIRST INVASION OF THE ARCTIC.

THE mysteries of the Arctic regions, and the special dangers inseparable from every attempt to solve them, seem always to have exercised a strange fascination over the minds of those who " go down to the sea in ships, and occupy their business in great waters."

The first of man's invasions of the far north were not deliberate, but accidental—the result of the storms at sea by which mariners, driven far out of their course to the northward, became aware of vast lands, bleak and inhospitable, covered with never-melting ice and snow. But the sight of those hitherto unknown solitudes roused in the minds of their first beholders a keen desire to explore them ; and so was first kindled that spirit of adventure which has led men ever since to dare so much in their efforts to overcome the obstacles in the way of the final solution of the problems of the Arctic.

Amongst the earliest of adventurous voyagers in northern seas whose expeditions led to practical results were the brothers Zeni, members of a noble Venetian family. The elder of them, Nicolo, started on his first voyage of discovery at the close of the fourteenth century. When he had got as far north as the Faroe Islands he was wrecked ; but he found a friend in the Earl of Orkney and Caithness, who took him into his service as pilot.

The Earl was interested in the desire of his *protégé* to reach the far north, and after a time sent him off, with his brother Antonio, on a voyage to Greenland. Mr. R. H. Major, F.S.A., one of the secretaries of the Royal Geographical Society, from the letters and journals—only partially preserved—of these courageous men, gathered that they reached their destination in safety, and found there much that interested, and doubtless astonished them. They discovered, for instance, a monastery of friars, preachers, and a church of St. Thomas, close by a volcanic hill. There was also a hot-water spring which the monks used for heating the church and the entire monastery, and by which they cooked their meat and baked their bread. By a judicious use of this hot water they raised in their small covered gardens the flowers, fruits and herbs of more temperate climates, thereby gaining much respect from their neighbours, who brought them presents of meat, chickens, etc. They were indebted, the narrative says, to the volcano for the very materials of their buildings ; for by throwing water on the burning stones while still hot, they converted them into a tenacious and indestructible substance, which they used as mortar.

"They have not much rain, as there is a settled frost all through their nine months' winter. They live on wild fowl and fish, which are attracted by the warmth of that part of the sea into which the hot water falls, and which forms a commodious harbour.

"The houses are built all round the hill, and are circular in form and tapering to the top, where there is a little hole for light and air ; the ground below supplying all necessary heat. In summer time they are visited by ships from neighbouring islands, and from Trondheim, which bring them corn, cloth and other necessaries, in exchange for fish and skins. Some of the monks are from Norway, Sweden and elsewhere, but most of them from Shetland. The harbour is generally full of vessels detained by the freezing of the sea, and waiting for the spring to melt the ice.

"The fishermen's boats are like a weaver's shuttle ; they are made of the skins of fish, and sewn together in such a manner that in bad weather the fisherman can fasten himself up in his boat and expose himself to the wind and sea without fear, for tney can stand a good many bumps without receiving any injury. In the bottom of the boat is a kind of sleeve tied fast in the middle, and when water gets into the boat they put it into one half of the sleeve, close it above with two pieces of wood, and loose the band beneath, so that the water runs out.

" The friars are liberal to workmen, and to those who bring them fruit and seeds, so that many resort to them. Most of the monks, especially the principals and superiors, speak the Latin language ; and this is all that is known of Engroneland (Greenland) as described by Messire Nicolo Zeno."

After Nicolo's death, his brother Antonio remained for some time in the service of the earl ; and he records the remarkable story of six fishermen who, being driven on to the shore of a new land in a gale, undoubtedly reached North America. "These men were brought by the natives into a large and populous city, and taken before the chief, who sent for many interpreters to speak with them ; but only one of those, who spoke Latin, and had also been cast by chance upon the island, could understand them." They remained some time in the country at the desire of the natives ; but ultimately they left them, and went to a distant part of this unknown land, and remained for thirteen years amongst a people who greatly respected them on account of their knowledge of various arts.

At length one of the fishermen escaped, and

succeeded in getting back to his own country. From the records of the adventure that remain, there is no doubt these men had been in America ; and their account of the people they met there gives conclusive proof that there were European settlers on the American continent at least a hundred years before the great voyage of Columbus—who, by the way, had visited both Iceland and Greenland before he found the New World.

The first serious attempt at the discovery of a north-west passage was made by the brothers Cabot, sons of a Venetian merchant who had settled in Bristol. One of them, Sebastian, relates how there was in his heart " a great flame of desire to attempt some notable thing ; and understanding," he says, " by reason of the sphere that if I should saile by way of the north-west, I should by a shorter tract come into India, I thereupon caused the King to be advertised of my desire, who immediately commanded two caravels to bee furnished with all things appertayning to the voyage, which was, as farre as I remember, in the year 1496, in the begining of summer. I began thereupon to saile toward the north-west, not thinking to find any other land than that of Cathay, and from thence to turn toward India. But after certaine dayes, I found that the land ranne toward the north. And seeing that at 56 degree under our pole the coast turned toward the east, despairing to find the passage, I turned backe again, and sailed downe by the coast of that land toward the equinoctiall (ever with interest to find the saide passage to India) and came to that part of the firme land which is now called Florida, where, my victuals failing, I departed from thence and returned unto England."

Thirty years before this adventure of Sebastian Cabot, and again in 1500, the Portuguese sent exploring parties into the northern seas. One result of these expeditions was a more complete knowledge of the Labrador and Newfoundland coasts; and to Gaspar Cortereal, who was in charge of the expedition of 1500, belongs the credit of having discovered Canada and the great St. Lawrence river. The Portuguese imagined at first that the mighty St. Lawrence was a strait, by which the long sought north-west passage would at last be found; and in their disappointment at finding that after all it was only a river, they exclaimed, " *Cà nada !* " (" Here, nothing,"), and thus gave to the great British colony the somewhat uncomplimentary name by which it has ever since been known.

The French and the Spaniards made various other unsuccessful attempts to explore the Arctic regions; and in 1527, Robert Thorne, another Bristol merchant, prevailed upon

Henry VIII. to despatch "two faire ships, well manned and victualled, having in them divers cunning men, to seek strange regions in the distant north." The expedition met with no success, for one of the "two faire ships" was lost, and the other returned without having achieved anything. But the venture of Robert Thorne is of special interest, since he is the first man known to have advocated definitely polar exploration. In an "exhortation" to the King concerning his expedition, he offers "very weighty and substantial reasons to set forth a discoverie *even to the North Pole.*" That is the earliest reference on record to the North Pole as the goal of an explorer's ambition; and during the long period of nearly four hundred subsequent years, the hope of reaching that goal never faded from the minds of men.

In 1576, Sir Martin Frobisher, one of the most famous of Arctic explorers, set out on the first of his three memorable voyages towards the north-west. He was a persistent advocate of Arctic exploration, and it took him fifteen years of persuasion to induce his friends to entrust him with funds sufficient for the purpose of his first voyage. He was a visionary, as well as an explorer; for he brought home from that first voyage some black stone which he supposed to contain gold, and such excitement followed his report of gold in the Arctic that no less than fifteen vessels set sail for the new land of gold, to which Queen Elizabeth gave the name of *Meta incognita*. But nothing save disappointment awaited the too sanguine voyagers; and the hundred persons who went out to form a settlement in the golden country returned, after encountering many perils from storms, fogs and ice, sadder and wiser men.

But if Frobisher was a failure as a gold prospector he was a brilliant success as a sailor, and his voyages resulted in a greatly increased knowledge of the Greenland coasts, straits and islands. Moreover, he fought bravely afterwards in the service of his country against the Spanish Armada. It is said of him that he was a man of enormous strength, and on one of his voyages an Esquimaux, attracted to the side of his vessel, was lifted bodily on board by Frobisher, " by maine force, boate and all !"

Seven years after Frobisher made his first voyage, Sir Humphrey Gilbert set sail to take possession of the northern parts of America and Newfoundland. Belief in the existence of mineral wealth in those regions was still strong, and one of the objects of Sir Humphrey's voyage was to find, if possible, further ground for this belief. The three vessels forming his expedition met with ill fortune. One of them was wrecked, but

Sir Humphrey escaped on the *Squirrel*, a
tiny bark of ten tons. The remaining vessel,
the *Golden Hinde*, was nearly swamped by a
huge wave, and when she righted herself
Sir Humphrey was observed shouting to the
sailors, and they heard him say, " Courage,
my lads !   We are as near to heaven by sea
as by land ! "   A few hours later his own
boat was swallowed up and all on board
perished.

But the great enterprise of the times was
still the discovery of the north-west passage ;
and in 1585 sundry London merchants again
" cast in their adventure," and sent out John
Davis with two ships named *Sunshine* and
Moonshine to see what he could do.   His
ships were well supplied with all necessary
equipments, and carried in addition " a band
of music to cheer and recreate the spirits of
the natives."   But though the voyagers had
an interesting and lively time amongst the
Esquimaux, little in the way of exploration
was accomplished ; and a second voyage,
which Davis undertook, with four ships, in the
following year was almost equally barren of
result. The seamen, hopeless at accomplishing
their purpose, and alarmed at the enormous
ice-floes which barred their progress, warned
their commander that " by his over-boldness
he might cause their widows and fatherless
children to give him bitter curses " ; and,
touched by their appeal, Davis sent one of

his ships home. With the boldest of his followers he himself pushed on in the *Moonshine* as far as the coast of Labrador, but here the treachery of the natives and stress of weather caused him to turn homewards.

Once again, in 1587, Davis set out northward in the *Sunshine*, accompanied by another vessel named the *E'izabeth*, and a pinnace. On this occasion the two larger vessels were required to engage in whaling at all suitable times, in order to reduce the expenses of the expedition ; and on reaching the coast of Greenland Davis went forward in the pinnace, leaving the other vessels to catch whales! He explored a good deal of the coast and sailed for two days up Cumberland Strait— which he had discovered during his first expedition ; but believing this passage to be an enclosed gulf he returned, and made for the point at which it had been arranged that the two whaling vessels should wait for him. But to his consternation and dismay, he discovered that his companions had basely deserted him. They had sailed away, leaving him to get home as best he could in his miserable pinnace. The voyage was a dangerous one to undertake in such a cockle shell, but he accomplished it in safety. He pleaded hard to be allowed to undertake yet another expedition ; but his previous efforts had proved so disappointing that his plea met with no response.

The next serious attempt at the achievement of the north-west passage was made by the ·Dutch, who, seven years after Davis's last Arctic voyage, sent three vessels on a voyage of northern discovery, under the general command of William Barentz, one of the most experienced seamen of the day. On reaching the coast of Lapland the vessels separated. Two of them shortly returned to Holland, while Barentz made his way to the most northern point of Nova Zembla. Shortly after this, however, ice gathered about the ship in such quantities as it lay near the shore that it was soon raised far above the level of the sea ; and the brave sailors had to face the fact that it was impossible to escape from their icy fastness before the next summer. Gerrit de Veer, who accompanied the expedition, relates that the men were " much grieved " at the prospect before them, of having " to live there all that cold winter, which we knew would fall out to be extremely bitter."

By great good fortune, the Dutchmen found a quantity of driftwood on the strand which served both for fuel and for the construction of a small hut. The finding of this wood was probably their salvation ; for without adequate shelter and means of warmth, they must have perished miserably in the dreary months that followed. The rigours of winter set in early, and by September the ground was frozen so hard that they were unable to

dig a grave for the burial of a comrade who
died, and it was only with utmost difficulty
that they contrived, with their numbed,
cramped fingers to build the hut.   It was the
middle of October before this task was accomplished.   The shelter was rude enough, but
they were thankful to have it.   In the middle
of it they built their fire, giving the warmest
place to one of their number who was ill ; and
they arranged their beds on shelves round
the walls.   The sun had now entirely disappeared, and they had entered upon a
night which would continue without a break
for long, weary months ; and, at the very
time when abundance of food was needed
to maintain the heat and health of the body,
they found that their daily rations of bread,
cheese and wine must be reduced.   Terrific
snowstorms, as well as cold and darkness,
made it impossible to leave their miserable
refuge even for needed exercise ; but by
setting traps close to the hut, they managed
to catch a good many Arctic foxes, and thus
secured a welcome supply of fresh food.

As the cold grew more intense, it is no
cause for wonder that their hearts failed them ;
and, as De Veer says, " we looked pitifully
one upon the other, being in great fear that
if the extremity of the cold grew to be more
and more, we should all die there of cold, for
that what fire soever we made would not
warm us."   How could it, indeed, with a

frost so keen and penetrating that there was a coating of ice two inches thick on the inside walls of the hut, and their very clothes, as they sat huddled round their wood fire, were whitened with frost ? But amid all their sufferings they never quite lost heart ; and there is something almost pathetic in the fact that, remembering January 5th was Twelfth Eve, they resolved to celebrate the occasion as well as they could. De Veer says : " We prayed our Maister that we might be merrie that night, and said that we were content to spend some of the wine that night which we had spared, and which was our share (one glass) every second day, and whereof for certaine days we had not dranke, and so that night we made merrie and drew for king. And therewith we had two pounds of meal, whereof we made pancakes with oyle, and every man had a white biscuit which we sopt in the wine. And so supposing that we were in our owne country and amongst our friends, it comforted us well as if we had made a great banquet in our owne house. And we also made trinkets, and our gunner was King of Nova Zembla, which is at least 800 miles long, and lyeth between two seas."

Towards the end of January, the sun made its appearance, to the great joy of the little company. The fury of the snowstorms also abated somewhat, so that exercise out-of-doors became possible, although the cold continued so extreme that the greatest care was necessary to avoid undue exposure. Bears now began to come about the hut, and some were shot, their grease affording welcome means of illumination, so that it was possible to burn lamps and pass the time in reading.

The bears had apparently a strong antipathy to these good Dutchmen, for their chronicle records more than one desperate and disastrous encounter with them. On the voyage northward, for instance, some of the crew had landed on an island to search for pieces of rock crystal. While two of them were kneeling on the shore, " a great leane white beare came sodainly stealing out and caught one of them fast by the necke, who, not knowing what it was, cried out and said, ' Who is it that pulles me so by the necke ? ' " His companion, seeing it was a " monsterous beare," ran away, leaving the other to fall a victim to the animal's ferocity. On another occasion—while they were building their house—a bear was shot dead while sampling the contents of a barrel of salt beef ; and at another time one of these creatures tried very hard to make close acquaintance with them— even attempting to enter their hut by the chimney !

With the return of summer the men made a determined effort to free their vessel from the ice. In this, however, they were unsuccessful, and their only hope of escape

A DESPERATE ENCOUNTER.

then rested on their two small boats; and on June 12th, 1596, they finally quitted the scene of their long and painful imprisonment. There were fifteen men in all when the boats set sail, and their provisions were reduced to a scanty supply of Dutch cheese, sea-biscuit, and wine. Thus, weakened by months of suffering and privation, and with an altogether inadequate supply of food, and with Barentz himself and one of the crew prostrate with sickness, this undaunted little company of brave men set out on their hazardous journey of 1,524 miles in two open boats, through an unknown sea, choked with ice, and very tempestuous. Their voyage has been truly described as one of the most adventurous ever made in the Arctic seas.

On the fourth day of their voyage the boats were hemmed in by enormous masses of floating ice, which so crushed and injured them that the crews gave up all hope of escape, and took solemn farewell of each other. In this crisis it was De Vee 5, by prompt and courageous action, foun vay of deliverance. With a well secured rope, he jumped from his boat to an ice block, then to another, and so on, until he reached a large floe, to which first the sick, then the stores, then the crews, and lastly the boats themselves were transferred. Here the party had to remain, while they repaired their damaged boats, and here the brave Barentz breathed his last.

His death was bitterly mourned by his comrades, to whom he had greatly endeared himself by his unselfishness and his devotion.

Deprived of their leader, the men were almost in despair; but still they bravely struggled on, contending, like the heroes they were, against sickness and semi-starvation, as well as against the perils inseparable from their surroundings. Several of them were nearly drowned; scurvy—the terrible sea-scourge of those days—broke out amongst them; bears attacked them; huge masses of grinding ice crushed the sides of their frail boats; they lost their goods, and part of their scanty store of provisions was spoilt by the water. But they never quite lost hope; day after day they persevered, and at last—on September 2nd—they reached Cola, a small seaport of Russian Lapland, where they received a joyous welcome from friends who had long since given them up for dead. Eight weeks later they were safe in their own homes in Holland, and they received at the hands of their countrymen a welcome such as only heroes deserve.

Nearly three centuries after the return of this brave company of Dutch adventurers, Captain Carlsen, while circumnavigating Nova Zembla, discovered the very house which they had built and in which they had spent that terrible winter of 1596; and within it he found many relics of the expedition. In a paper read before the Royal Geographical Society in 1873, Mr. C. R. Markham, commenting upon this most interesting discovery, said, " No man had entered the lonely dwelling where the famous discoverer of Spitzbergen had sojourned during the long winter of 1596, for nearly three centuries. There stood the cooking-pan over the fire-place, the old clock against the wall, the arms, the tools, the drinking-vessels, the instruments, and the books that had beguiled the weary hours of that long night two hundred and seventy seven years ago. Perhaps the most touching relic of all is the pair of small shoes. There was a little cabin-boy among the crew, who died, as Gerrit de Veer tells us, during the winter. This accounts for the shoes having been left behind. There is a flute, too, once played by that poor boy, which will still give out a few notes." The relics were brought home by Captain Carlsen, and are now preserved at the Hague.

CHAPTER II.

THE merchants of London, who had persevered so long and spent money so lavishly in their efforts to discover either a north-west or a north-east passage, now determined to see whether they could not effect their purpose by exploration directly towards the North Pole. With this object in view they fitted out an expedition in 1607, and appointed Henry Hudson commander. He set sail in a vessel hopelessly small and ill-fitted for the work, with a crew of only ten men and a boy. To the north of Spitzbergen he found further progress impossible, owing to the ice which threatened swift destruction to his small craft. So he turned back, and reached London again safely, beaten, but by no means discouraged, and in the following year he set out again, this time towards the north-east. But once more he failed. Still undeterred, he made a third attempt in 1609, in the service of the Dutch, pursuing this time a somewhat erratic course, which ended in the discovery of the beautiful river at whose mouth New York is now situated.

In 1610 he made his fourth and last venture, which terminated in a cruel tragedy that cost England the service of one of her bravest and most intrepid sons. It was during this voyage that Hudson entered the great bay or sea which has ever since borne his name, and thus opened up the most valuable fur trade in the world. The vessel in which this final expedition was made became ice-bound on the coast of Labrador, and threats of mutiny were heard amongst the crew. But, notwithstanding this, Hudson determined to continue his voyage as soon as the ship was free. This he did, but misfortune followed him; the mutinous mutterings of the crew developed into open rebellion; and at last, when provisions began to fail, the mutineers seized their commander, tied his hands behind his back, hustled him into a boat with "seven sick and lame men," threw in a little provender, and then cut the boat adrift, leaving it and its eight helpless occupants at the mercy of ice and sea.

Nothing more was ever heard of poor Hudson, who thus perished miserably, the victim of one of the most cruel acts of treachery on record in connection with Arctic exploration. Retribution quickly overtook the wretched men responsible for his death, for most of them died of starvation or were killed in quarrels with the natives; and the few who survived had to endure the agonies of extreme privation before they succeeded in reaching civilization.

Of all that dastardly crew, only one man remained true to his master—John King, the ship's carpenter. His name deserves to be held in honourable remembrance; for when Hudson was lowered into the boat, he insisted on following him, and thus paid for his fidelity with his life.

The report of the discovery of Hudson's Bay gave a new impetus to Arctic exploration, and many fresh expeditions were organized, in the hope of discovering somewhere on the western shore of the great Bay the passage which should open the way to India. All such hopes were of course doomed to disappointment, and Baffin, who sailed in 1616, and discovered the entrances to Smith's, Jones' and Lancaster Sounds, was so firmly persuaded that they were merely enclosed gulfs, that he did not trouble to explore them; and his theory was so generally accepted that for nearly two centuries no further attempt was made to discover a western passage in this direction.

In the year 1619 the Danes entered the field, and Christian IV. fitted out two vessels for a voyage of northern discovery, under the command of Jens Munk. This wise navigator chose his crew mostly from English sailors

ABANDONED! THE TRAGEDY OF HUDSON.

who had already had experience of Arctic voyages. The venture, however, proved disastrous. With the approach of winter, Munk was compelled to seek shelter on land for his company of sixty-four souls, and he constructed huts in which they did their best to defy the cold. But their efforts were not altogether successful. Before the winter ended scurvy attacked them ; they became so weak that they were unable even to obtain the ducks and geese which flocked around them, and many of them died.

When the winter was over the only survivors of the party were Munk himself and two of his crew. Munk, though prostrate with disease, exerted himself to collect herbs and plants which, to some extent, counteracted the effects of the scurvy ; and at last, with the help of the two men, contrived to equip the smaller of his vessels with stores and appliances from the larger one and set sail.

The three poor fellows, making their last desperate struggle for life, were so ill that they could do little but let their vessel drift across the stormy sea ; but hope grew stronger as every moment brought them nearer to safety, and at last, on September 25th, 1620, they reached the coast of Norway. They had long been given up by their friends for dead, and their return was looked upon as little short of miraculous. They were greeted with greatest enthusiasm, and so strongly was

Munk moved by the interest and sympathy of his countrymen, that, in spite of his terrible experiences, he proposed a second voyage. His proposal was received with acclamation, and when all was ready Munk went to court to take leave of the king. There he met with an unexpected rebuff, for he was warned to be careful, and the king apparently blamed him for the failure and loss of life that had attended his first attempt. So acutely did the brave old sailor feel this undeserved rebuke that he forgot himself for the moment, and answered the king in language hardly in accord with court etiquette. Whereupon, the story goes, the monarch also so far forgot his dignity as to strike Munk with his cane. The incident so rankled in the sailor's mind that he became ill, took to his bed, and, so report says, died soon afterwards of a broken heart.

Other Arctic voyagers of the seventeenth century include Captain Luke Foxe—an altogether irresponsible explorer who achieved nothing, and who says of his enterprise that he " made but a scurvie voyage of it "— Captain Danells—a Dane—and Captains Gillam, Wood and Flawes. Their adventures were all more or less unfortunate, and they added little to the geographical knowledge gained by their predecessors.

The first notable Arctic voyage of the eighteenth century was that of James Knight, head man of the Hudson's Bay Company's factory, or trading port, on Nelson's River. In his intercourse with the native Indians, Knight had learned that there was a rich deposit of copper near a navigable river to the north of their station. So impressed was he with the possibilities of this copper deposit, that he came to England and induced the company to organize an expedition, of which he was placed in charge. Two vessels were fitted out, and left Gravesend in the spring of 1719, Knight's instructions being to attempt a north-west passage, as well as to search for minerals. But the ill-fated vessels never returned ; and for forty-eight years the fate of Knight and the men who accompanied him remained a mystery. Then, in 1767, near Marble Island, some of the Company's employees discovered in a harbour the remains of a house, guns, anchors, a smith's anvil, and other articles ; while further search revealed the hulls of the two ships below the water. With the assistance of a native interpreter in the service of the company, the following particulars were gleaned from some aged Esquimaux living near. The information, which is taken from a work by Samuel Hearne, gives a painfully graphic idea of the terrible straits to which these unfortunate men were reduced before death mercifully released them from their sufferings :

" When the vessels arrived at this place (Marble Island) it was very late in the fall, and in getting them into the harbour the largest received much damage ; but on being fairly in, the English began to build the house, their number at that time seeming to be about fifty. As soon as the ice permitted, in the following summer, 1720, the Esquimaux paid them another visit, by which time the number of the English was very greatly reduced, and those that were living seemed very unhealthy. According to the account given by the Esquimaux, they were then very busily employed, but about what they could not easily describe—probably in lengthening the long-boat, for, at a little distance from the house, there was now lying a great quantity of oak chips, which had been made most assuredly by the carpenters.

" A sickness and famine occasioned such havoc among the English that by the setting in of the second winter their number was reduced to twenty. That winter, 1720, some of the Esquimaux took up their abode on the opposite side of the harbour to that on which the English had built their houses, and frequently supplied them with such provisions as they had, which consisted chiefly of whale's blubber, seal's flesh and train oil. When the spring advanced, the Esquimaux went to the continent, and on their visiting Marble Island again, in the summer of 1721, they only found five of the English alive ; and those were in such distress for provisions that they eagerly ate the seal's flesh and whale's blubber quite raw as they purchased it from the natives.

" This disordered them so much that three of them died in a few days, and the other two, though very weak, made ⌐ ⌐hift to bury them. These two survived n. ⌐ays after the rest, and frequently went ⌐ ' ⌐ top of an adjacent rock and earnestly looked to the south and east as if in expectation of some vessels coming to their relief. After continuing there a considerable time together, and nothing appearing in sight, they sat down close together and wept bitterly. At length one of the two died, and the other's strength was so far exhausted that he fell down and died also in attempting to dig a grave for his companion. The skulls and other large bones of those two men are now lying above ground close to the house. The longest liver was, according to the Esquimaux account, always employed in working iron into implements for them ; probably he was the armourer or smith."

No further serious attempt to per⌐trate the Arctic Circle was made until Peter the Great decided to have a thorough exploration of the whole of the northern coast of Siberia. A few days before his death, the Czar summoned Vitus Bering, a Dane in the Russian service, and a man of exceptional ability and energy, to appear before him, and to him the monarch entrusted the difficult task of discovering

whether America and Asia were one, or how
closely their coasts approached. After the
Czar's death the Empress Catharine confirmed
the commands of her deceased husband, and
Bering, assisted by two lieutenants, Martin
Spanberg and Alexei Tschirikoff, set out from
St. Petersburg on February 5th, 1725, for the
Ochotsk Sea. So difficult was the Russian
overland route in those days, that it took the
explorers more than two years to transport
their outfit to Ochotsk, whence they crossed
to Bolcheretsk in a vessel specially built for
them. From there, during the following
year, they transported their provisions and
stores to Nijni, and on July 10th, 1728, they
set out in a vessel named the *Gabriel*. After
two voyages in this ship, during which he
accomplished nothing of note, save the discovery of the straits which now bear his name,
Bering returned to St. Petersburg.

In 1741—on July 4th—he again set sail,
this time from Petropaulovski, with Tschirikoff
in charge of a second vessel. They had not
been long at sea when they encountered a
terrible storm, which separated them. Bering
made a few unimportant discoveries, and had
many adventures with the natives; but
scurvy made its appearance amongst his crew,
and Bering was compelled to abandon all
thought of further exploration. He turned
back, intending to make the coast of Kamschatka, but the voyage was one of extreme

difficulty owing to the increasing sickness amongst the crew. So weak were they that " two sailors who used to be at the rudder were obliged to be led in by two others, who could hardly walk. And when one could sit and steer no longer, another in little better condition supplied his place. Many sails they durst not hoist, because there was nobody to lower them in case of need."

When at last land was sighted, they decided to make for it ; but almost as soon as they had dropped anchor a storm arose, which drove their vessel on to the rocks. They cast another anchor, but the cable broke under the strain, and their vessel was pitched right over the rocks by a tremendous sea. Behind the rocks, however, they found themselves in comparatively calm water ; and, after having rested awhile, some of the crew succeeded in launching a boat, in which they reached the shore. They found themselves on an island, to which the name of their commander was given, and at once set to work to prepare a shelter of some kind for their sick comrades. They could find no timber, so, instead of building a house, they roofed in some ravines ; and " on the 8th of November, a beginning was made to land the sick ; but some died as soon as they were brought from between decks in the open-air ; others during the time they were on the deck, some in the boat, and many more as soon as they were brought on shore."

Bering himself was brought ashore in a dying condition the following day, and in spite of the unremitting care of his crew, who were devoted to him, he died on the island a month later.

The men who lived through that terrible time had to stand by, helpless, and watch the total wrecking of their vessel, and they suffered also the loss of nearly all their provisions. But with that dogged, determined heroism which a forced sojourn in the Arctic regions seems to breed in men, they contrived to construct a small vessel from the wreck of the old one, subsisting meanwhile on dead whales which had been driven inshore. In their new craft they ventured to put to sea, and at length reached the coast of Kamschatka.

CHAPTER III.

AFTER a comparatively long interval, during which no specially notable effort was made to invade the realm of the ice-king, polar exploration received in 1818 a tremendous impetus by a remarkable break-up of the vast barrier of ice on the eastern coast of Old Greenland, and its re-appearance in a more southerly latitude. So many navigators reported this independently that it was generally regarded as a fact too well authenticated to admit of doubt ; and scientific men of the day advanced the theory that with the disappearance of this great barrier it might be found that the chief obstacle to the discovery of a north-west route to the Pacific had been removed.

In order that this theory might be practically tested, the then Prince Regent, afterwards King George IV., agreed that two attempts should be made to reach the Pacific by different routes, and the command of the first expedition which undertook the task of attempting to achieve this feat by the north-west passage was entrusted to Captain John Ross. Although many notable scientific and naval men accompanied Ross —amongst them Parry, who afterwards proved himself an able and zealous Arctic explorer—the results were most meagre and disappointing.

The second expedition was no less remarkable than that of Ross, in regard to its *personnel.* Its commander was Captain David Buchan, who had already made his mark as a fearless traveller, having but recently returned from a land journey across Newfoundland in order to interview the natives—a feat which no European had previously attempted. Amongst his colleagues on the Arctic expedition were Franklin, who had an associate command, Beechey, Back, and many other distinguished men of the day. Like Parry, however, he failed to achieve his object, which was to reach the North Pole by way of Spitzbergen. He made many gallant attempts to overcome the difficulties in the way ; but ultimately, owing to the damage his vessels had sustained through the grinding and pounding of the ice, he was compelled to return home.

Some of the dangers encountered in the course of the expedition were afterwards graphically described by Beechey, who, amongst other thrilling stories, gives the following account of the fall of an avalanche from the end of a glacier :

" It was occasioned by the discharge of a musket at about half a mile distance from the glacier. Immediately after the report of the gun, a noise resembling thunder was heard in the direction of the glacier, and in a few seconds more an immense piece broke away and fell headlong into the sea. The crew of the launch, supposing themselves to be beyond the reach of its influence, quietly looked upon the scene, when presently a sea arose and rolled towards the shore with such rapidity that the crew had not time to take any precautions, and the boat was in consequence washed up on the beach and completely filled by the succeeding wave. As soon as their astonishment had subsided they examined the boat, and found her so badly stove that it became necessary to repair her in order to return to the ship. They had also the curiosity to measure the distance the boat had been carried by the wave, and found it to be ninety-six feet.

" A second discharge occurred on a remarkably fine day, when the quietness of the bay was first interrupted by the noise of the falling body. Lieutenant Franklin and myself had approached one of these stupendous walls of ice, and were endeavouring to search into the innermost recess of a deep cavern that was near the foot of the glacier, when we heard a report, as if of a cannon, and turning to the quarter whence it proceeded, we perceived an immense piece of the front of the glacier sliding down from the height of two hundred feet at least into the sea, and dispersing the water in every direction, accompanied by a loud grinding noise, and followed by a quantity of water, which, being previously lodged in the fissures, now made its escape in numberless small cascades over the front of the glacier.

" The piece that had been disengaged at first wholly disappeared under water, and nothing was seen but a violent boiling of the sea and a shooting up of clouds of spray, like that which occurs at the foot of a great cataract. After a short time it re-appeared, raising its head full a hundred feet above the surface, with water pouring down from all parts of it ; and then, labouring, as if doubtful which way it should fall, it rolled over, and after rocking about for some minutes, at length became settled.

" We now approached it, and found it nearly a quarter of a mile in circumference and sixty feet out of the water. Knowing its specific gravity, and making a fair allowance for its inequalities, we computed its weight at 421,660 tons. A stream of salt water was still pouring down its sides, and there was a continual cracking noise, as loud as that of a cart-whip, occasioned, I suppose, by the escape of fixed air."

Undismayed by the comparative failure of all previous attempts at Arctic exploration, Captain Parry, already a naval officer of considerable distinction, accepted, in 1819, the command of a new expedition, the object of which was to accomplish what his immediate predecessors had failed to do. Two vessels were placed at his disposal, the *Hecla* and *Griper*. The first of these was under his own command, and the second was in charge of Lieutenant Liddin.

When they reached the south side of Melville Island, the vessels became ice-locked and so they remained for ten months. This is a condition almost inevitable to any vessel that passes a winter in the Arctic circle, and Parry, in his journal, gives the following interesting description of the process by which progress is first impeded and finally stopped altogether. It begins by the formation of " young " ice upon the surface of the sea as winter approaches, and Parry states 'hat this formation " is the circumstance which most decidedly begins to put a stop to the navigation of these seas, and warns the seaman that his season of active operations is nearly at an end. It is, indeed, scarcely possible to conceive the degree of hindrance occasioned by this impediment, trifling as it always appears before it is encountered.

" When the sheet has acquired the thickness of about half an inch, and is of considerable extent, a ship is liable to be stopped by it, unless favoured by a strong and free wind; and even when retaining her way through the water at the rate of a mile an hour, her course is not always under the control of the helmsman, though assisted by the wisest attention to the action of the sails; but it depends upon some accidental increase or decrease in the thickness of the sheet of ice with which one bow or the other comes in contact. Nor is it possible in this situation for the boats to render their usual assistance by running out lines or otherwise; for, having once entered the young ice, they can only be propelled slowly through it by digging the oars and boat-hooks into it, at the same time breaking it across the bows, and by rolling the boat from side to side.

" After continuing this laborious work for some time with little good effect, and considerable damage to the planks and oars, a boat is often obliged to return the same way that she came, backing out in the canal thus formed to no purpose.

" A ship in this helpless state, her sails in vain expanded to a favourable breeze, her ordinary resources failing, and suddenly arrested in her course upon the element through which she has been accustomed to move without restraint, has often reminded me of Gulliver tied down by the feeble hands of Lilliputians; nor are the struggles she makes to effect a release, and the apparent insignificance of the means by which her efforts are opposed, the least just or the least vexatious part of the resemblance."

Captain Parry's chief concern, on finding that any movement of the ships was out of the question for a very long period, seems to have been for the amusement and well-being of the men for whom he was responsible. " Under circumstances of leisure and inactivity such as we were now placed in," he says, " and with every prospect of its continuance for a very large portion of the year, I was desirous of finding some amusement for the men during this long and tedious interval. I proposed, therefore, to the officers to get up a play occasionally on board the *Hecla,* as the readiest means of preserving among our crew that cheerfulness and good humour which had hitherto subsisted.

" In this proposal I was readily seconded by the officers of both ships, and Lieutenant Beechey having been duly elected as stage manager, our first performance was fixed for the 5th of November, to the great delight of the ships' companies. In these amusements I gladly took a part myself, considering that an example of cheerfulness, by giving a direct countenance to everything that could con-tribute to it, was not the least essential part of my duty, under the peculiar circumstances in which we were placed.

" In order still further to promote good

humour among ourselves, as well as to furnish amusing occupation during the hours of constant darkness, we set on foot a weekly newspaper which was to be called the *North Georgia Gazette and Winter Chronicle*, and of which Captain Sabine undertook to be the editor, under the promise that it was to be supported by original contributions from the officers of the two ships."

In these and other ways Parry contrived to keep his men occupied and interested through the dreary monotony of the Arctic winter ; but the mild excitements the commander provided were as nothing compared with that which accident gave them, when a fire broke out in their house on shore. In their eagerness to save their instruments and other valuables from the flames several of the crew were severely frost-bitten ; and some idea of the intensity of the cold which causes this calamity may be gathered from the fact that when one of the men plunged his frosted hand into a basin of cold water, the surface of the water became instantly frozen through the sudden lowering of the temperature.

Not until the following August was Parry able to release his vessels from their icy prison, and the release was accompanied by dangers and difficulties greater even than those which were encountered at the beginning of the previous winter. Captain Lyon, who was associated with the commander in this expedition, thus describes the critical situation of the *Hecla :*

" The flood-tide, coming down with a more than ordinary quantity of ice, pressed the ship very much, and rendered it necessary to run out the stream cable, in addition to the hawsers which were fast to the land ice. This was scarcely accomplished when a very heavy and extensive floe took the ship on her broadside, and, being backed by another large body of ice, gradually lifted her stern as if by the action of a wedge.

" The weight every moment increasing obliged us to veer on the hawsers, whose friction was so great as nearly to cut through the bilt-heads, and ultimately set them on fire, so that it became requisite for people to attend with buckets of water. The pressure was at length too powerful for resistance ; and the stream cable, with two six and one five inch hawsers, went at the same moment. Three others soon followed. The sea was too full of ice to allow the ship to drive, and the only way by which she could yield to the enormous weight which oppressed her was by leaning over the land ice, while her stern at the same time was entirely lifted more than five feet out of the water.

" The lower deck beams now complained very much, and the whole frame of the ship underwent a trial which would have proved fatal to any less strengthened vessel. At this

moment the rudder was unhung with a
sudden jerk, which broke up the rudder-case
and struck the driver-boom with great force.
In this state I made known our situation
by telegraph, as I clearly saw that, in the
event of another floe backing the one which
lifted us, the ship must inevitably turn over,
or part in midships. The pressure which had
been so dangerous at length proved our
friend ; for by its increasing weight the floe
on which we were borne burst upwards,
unable to resist its force. The ship righted,
and, a small slack opening in the water,
drove several miles to the southward before
she could again be secured to get the rudder
hung ; circumstances much to be regretted
at the moment, as our people had been
employed, with but little intermission, for
three days and nights, attending to the safety
of the ship in this dangerous tideway."

But at length both ships were free from the
ice, and Parry set sail for England, which he
reached safely with all his crew—except one
man who had died of an incurable disease—
but with very meagre results to show for all
the dangers and hardships he had so bravely
and cheerfully faced.

A year or two later Captain Lyon, Parry's
associate on his first expedition, set sail for
the far north. His object was not so much
Arctic discovery as the completion of the
survey of the northernmost coasts of America;

but his effort is worthy of record in these pages
because of the striking example it affords of
the heroism and devoutness of brave men
under conditions of extreme peril. Lyon had
the misfortune to sail in a vessel scarcely sea-
worthy and wholly unfitted for the strain of
service in the Arctic regions. Almost as
soon as she reached the ice the troubles of her
captain began ; and when a gale sprang up
and the ship was driving helplessly before it
towards a shore on which huge breakers were
dashing with thunderous roar, everyone on
board felt that disaster and death were
imminent. All that the captain could do was
to direct his men to put on their warmest
garments in order that if they reached land
they might have the best possible chance of
life.

The sailors—forty, all told—brought their
kit bags on deck and proceeded to dress themselves in accordance with the captain's
instructions ; " and," he says, " in the fine
athletic forms which stood exposed before us,
I did not see one muscle quiver, nor the
slightest sign of alarm. And now that
everything in our power had been done, I
called all hands aft, and to a merciful God
offered prayers for our preservation. I
thanked everyone for their excellent conduct,
and cautioned them, as we should, in all
probability, soon appear before our Maker,
to enter His presence as men resigned to

their fate. Noble as the character of the
British sailor is always allowed to be in cases of
danger, yet I did not believe it to be possible
that, among forty-one persons, not one
repining word should have been uttered. The
officers sat about wherever they could find
shelter from the sea, and the men lay down
conversing with each other with the most
perfect calmness. Each was at peace with
his neighbour and with all the world ; and I
am firmly persuaded that the resignation
which was then shown to the will of the
Almighty was the means of obtaining His
mercy. God *was* merciful to us, and the
tide almost miraculously fell no lower."
Their deliverance from this danger gave them
fresh courage, and after many further perils
and vicissitudes they reached England safely.

Meanwhile Parry, undismayed by his
previous comparative failures, made further
attempts to solve the Arctic mystery ; and
in 1827 he set out on his fourth and final, and
in some respects most notable, expedition
to the north. This time, encouraged by
reports of previous explorers of great stretches
of smooth, unbroken ice to the north of
Spitzbergen, he determined to attempt to
reach the North Pole by means of sledge-
borne boats. Two of these boats were used.
They were specially constructed, made as
strong as possible to resist hard usage, and
fitted with every necessity for the work of the

FACING DEATH WITH A PRAYER.

explorers. The equipment included a bamboo mast, nineteen feet long, a tarred duck-sail, which could also be used as an awning, a boat-hook, fourteen paddles and a steering oar. The crew of each boat consisted of two officers and twelve men ; and the weight of each, with all its stores and appliances, was 3,753 pounds, exclusive of four sledges, each of which weighed twenty-six pounds.

With provisions for seventy-one days, Parry set out to the north of Spitzbergen with his boats and sledges, and he thus describes the general plan of travel he adopted :

" Our plan of travelling being nearly the same throughout this excursion after we first entered upon the ice, I may at once give some account of our usual mode of proceeding. It was my intention to travel wholly by night, and to rest by day, there being, of course, constant daylight in these regions during the summer season. The advantage of this plan, which was occasionally deranged by circumstances, consisted first in our avoiding the intense and oppressive glare from the snow during the time of the sun's greatest altitude, so as to prevent in some degree the painful inflammation in the eyes, called ' snow-blindness,' which is common in all snowy countries. We also thus enjoyed greater warmth during the hours of rest, and had a better chance of drying our clothes ; besides which, no small advantage was derived from the snow being harder at night for travelling. The only disadvantage of this plan was that the fogs were sometimes more frequent and more thick by night than by day, though even in this respect there was less difference than might have been supposed, the temperature during the twenty-four hours undergoing but little variation.

" This travelling by night and sleeping by day so completely inverted the natural order of things that it was difficult to persuade ourselves of the reality. Even the officers and myself, who were all furnished with pocket chronometers, could not always bear in mind at what part of the twenty-four hours we had arrived, and there were several of the men who declared, and I believe truly, that they never knew night from day during the whole excursion."

Progress was by no means so easy as Parry had supposed it would be. He knew he would· encounter a certain amount of danger and difficulty, but he had relied upon finding a fairly level and continuous field of ice on which to proceed ; and he had been led to expect this from explicit statements made by more than one of his predecessors in Arctic enterprises. Lutwidge, for instance, in 1773, reported that " one continued plain of smooth, unbroken ice, bounded only by the horizon,"· lay to the north of Spitzbergen ; and Scoresby spoke of the same thing in these emphatic

words : " I once saw a field that was so free
from either fissure or hummock, that I
imagine, had it been free from snow, a coach
might have been driven many leagues over
it in a direct line without obstruction or
danger."

Probably these explorers had not been near
enough to the actual icefield to be able to give
an accurate description of it. Certain it is
that when Parry reached it, instead of a plain
as level and smooth as a coach road, he found
a rough, hummocky surface, with countless
rugged masses of loose ice, interspersed with
pools of water. These obstructions sometimes necessitated three and even four journeys
over the same ground with their baggage, and
the   had often to be launched across the
poolboats

Frequently the crew had to go on hands and
knees to secure a footing. Heavy showers of
rain rendered the surface of the ice a mass of
slush, and in some places the ice took the form
of sharp-pointed crystals, which cut the boots
like penknives.

As may be imagined, the party made but
slow progress under such adverse conditions,
and the work proved to be extremely exhausting. Nor the least trying part of their
ordeal was the terrible monotony of their
surroundings.

In this connection Parry says : " As soon
as we arrived at the other end of the floe, or

came to any difficult place, we mounted one of the highest hummocks of ice near at hand (many of which were fifteen to twenty-five feet above the sea), in order to obtain a better view around us, and nothing could well exceed the dreariness which such a view presented. The eye wearied itself in vain to find an object but ice and sky to rest upon; and even the latter was often hid from our view by the dense and dismal fogs which so generally prevailed. For want of variety the most trifling circumstances engaged a more than ordinary share of our attention; a passing gull, a mass of ice of unusual form, became objects which our situation and circumstances magnified into ridiculous importance; and we have since often smiled to remember the eager interest with which we regarded many insignificant occurrences.

" It may well be imagined, then, how cheering it was to turn from this scene of inanimate desolation to our two little boats in the distance, to the moving figures of our men winding with their sledges among the hummocks, and to hear once more the sound of human voices breaking the stillness of this icy wilderness. In some cases Lieutenant Ross and myself took separate routes to try the ground, which kept us almost continually floundering among deep snow and water. The sledges having been brought up as far as we had explored, we all went back for the boats ; each boat's crew, when the road was tolerable, dragging their own, and the officers labouring equally hard with the men. It was thus that we proceeded for nine miles out of every ten that we travelled over ice, for it was very rarely indeed that we met with a surface sufficiently level and hard to drag all our loads at one journey, and in a great many instances during the first fortnight we had to make three journeys with the boats and baggage ; that is, to traverse the same road five times over."

In spite of the difficulties of the way Parry pushed on, hoping always that the conditions of travel would improve as they proceeded. How great those difficulties were will be understood when it is stated that they were once two hours in covering 150 yards ; and it was quite a common experience for them to have to journey ten or eleven miles to gain four miles to the northward.

After one exceptionally trying day, Parry says : " we determined to continue to the last our utmost exertions, though we could never once encourage the men by assuring them of our making good progress; and, setting out at seven in the evening, soon found that our hope of having permanently reached better ice was not to be realized ; for the floe on which we had slept was so full of hummocks that it occupied us just six hours to cross it, the distance in a straight line not exceeding two-miles-and-a-half."

For five long and weary weeks Parry persevered against the difficulties that beset him, and then, after thirty-five days of incessant drudgery, he was forced to recognise that he was beaten.

The discovery was made that while they were apparently advancing towards the pole, the icefield on which they were travelling was drifting towards the south, and thus rendering all their exertions fruitless. Yet, though disappointed in his hope of planting his country's standard on the northern axis of the globe, Parry had the glory of reaching the highest authenticated latitude until that time attained.

There was nothing for it now but to return ; and bitterly disappointed at his failure to attain his ambition, he began his journey back to the ship. Even now the trials of the brave little company of explorers were not at an end ; for on the northern coast of Spitzbergen the boats encountered a terrible storm on the open sea, which compelled them to make for Walden Island—one of the most northerly rocks of the archipelago—where, fortunately, a reserve supply of provisions had been deposited.

"Everything belonging to us," said Parry, " was now completely drenched by the spray and snow ; we had been fifty-six hours

without rest, and forty-eight a wor in tl
boats, so that by the time they were unloade
we had barely strength to haul th m up on the
rocks. However, by dint of great exertion,
we managed to get the boats above the surf,
after which, a hot supper, a blazing fire of
driftwood, and a few hours' quiet, restored us."
Ultimately the ship was reached in safety,
after an absence of sixty-one days.

The failure of Parry's main enterprise, so
bravely undertaken and so heroically pursued
under almost overwhelming difficulties, was
distinctly his misfortune, and not his fault.
He at least thoroughly deserved the success
he could not command, and between the
lines of his own modest summary of his
brave endeavour it is easy to read that he was
a man who knew how to endure, and who was
only driven at the last to accept failure out
of consideration for the lives of those who
trusted to his leadership. "The distance
traversed during this excursion," he say
" five hundred and sixty-nine geograpl al
miles; but, allowing for the number of times
had to return for our baggage during the
ater part of the journeys over the ice, we
timated our actual travelling at nine hundred
nd seventy-eight geographical, or eleven
undred and twenty-seven statute miles.
Considering our constant exposure to wet cold,
and fatigue, our stockings having generally
been drenched in snow-water for twelve hours

out of every four-and-twenty, I had great reason to be thankful for the excellent health in which, upon the whole, we reached the ship.''

It has been said with truth that the epoch of modern discoveries in the Arctic regions began with Parry; and in the long list of heroes of the frozen north no name is more worthy of honour than his.

CHAPTER IV.

A FIVE YEARS' BATTLE FOR FREEDOM.

IT seems to be a characteristic of all adventurers into the Arctic and Antarctic seas that failure never daunts them. When they find they cannot accomplish what they set out to achieve they do not give way to despondency. If at first they don't succeed, they try, try, try again. That is one of the outstanding features of all exploratory work in the polar seas; and amid all the stirring story of bravery and perseverance which that work affords, there is no finer example of courageous persistence than in the record of the second Arctic voyage of Captain John Ross.

The first voyage of Ross in 1818, as stated in the previous chapter, had been a failure. He had been appointed by the Government to the command of the *Isabella*, with instructions to proceed up the middle of Davis' Strait to a high northern latitude, and then to stretch across to the westward, in the hope of being able to pass the northern extremity of America and reach Behring's Strait by that

route. But he did little save establish
the accuracy of Baffin's surveys of the Bay
which bears his name. Proceeding further to
Lancaster Sound he was arrested by a curious
atmospheric deception of a range of mountains
apparently extending right across the passage.
So convinced was he of the reality of these
mountains that he refused to go any further ;
and to the dismay and disappointment of
his officers—of whom Parry was one—he
turned his ship about and made for home. It
was a sorry ending to what had been a most
promising expedition, and Ross was blamed
severely. But as his biographer says, the
best thing a man can do after having lost his
character is to do all he can to retrieve it ;
and it was not to be expected that Captain
Ross could sit tamely down with all the load
of obloquy upon his shoulders, and not make
some attempt to remove it. He had to wait
a long time for his opportunity, but at last
it came. In 1829—ten years after his first
failure—he was enabled, through the generous
help of Sir Felix Booth, to organize another
expedition. A small paddle steamer, named
the *Victory*, was purchased. Hitherto the
navigation of the Arctic seas had only been
attempted in sailing vessels ; and the idea of
taking paddle boxes amongst the ice floes was
regarded by experienced navigators of those
days as a huge mistake—as indeed, it proved
to be. But Ross was determined, and he

had his own way in the matter. He chose
for the second in command of his expedition
his nephew, Commander James Ross, and his
choice proved a wise one ; for he it was who
by his successful sledge journeys made the
chief discoveries of the expedition.

On May 23rd, 1829, the vessel set sail from
Woolwich on a voyage which was destined to
last five years. Long before that time had
elapsed Ross and all who were with him had
been given up for lost—and, indeed, his
expedition is even more remarkable in the
history of Arctic exploration for the time it
occupied than for its successes.

During the journey northward a severe gale
was encountered, and this so damaged the ship
that it was necessary to put in at the Danish
settlement of Holsteinberg, on the Greenland
coast, for repairs. But the adventurers were
soon under weigh again, and in August they
found themselves amongst the formidable
streams, packs and floating bergs of ice which
had offered such obstructions to Parry's
ships. On August 13th they reached the
spot where the *Fury* had been abandoned.
Of the vessel itself not a trace remained, but
all her sails, stores and provisions were found
just as Parry and his men had left them. The
hermetically sealed tin canisters had kept
all the provisions safe from the attacks of
the white bears ; and the flour, meat, bread,
sugar, wine, spirits, etc., were in as good

condition as when they were first packed. A great part of this store was appropriated by Ross, who thus increased his stock to two years and ten months' supply; and it was this providential " find " that enabled him and his party to live through the four long, terrible winters that lay before them.

Two days later Cape Garry, the farthest point seen by Parry on his third voyage, was reached; and here the *Victory* suffered severely through the buffettings of floating ice, and was greatly inconvenienced by dense fogs. Often their only safety lay in mooring the vessel to one of the mountains of ice that drifted around them ; and it was a wonder to them all that in spite of the constant bombardment by huge ice floes as hard as rock, the vessel sustained little damage.

Commander Ross gives a vivid description of what a vessel endures when sailing amongst these hills of moving ice. " Imagine," he says, " these mountains of ice, as solid as granite, hurled through a narrow strait by a rapid tide, meeting with the noise of thunder, breaking from each other's precipices huge fragments, or rending each other asunder, till, losing their former equilibrium, they fall over headlong, lifting the sea around in breakers and whirling it in eddies. There is not a moment in which it can be conjectured what will happen in the next; there is not one which may not be the last. The attention is troubled to fix on anything amid such confusion; still must it be alive that it may seize on the single moment of help or escape which may occur. Yet with all this, and it is the hardest task of all, there is nothing to be acted, no effort to be made. He must be patient, as if he were unconcerned, or careless, waiting as he can for the fate, be it what it may, which he cannot influence or avoid."

But in spite of all obstacles, Ross moved slowly forward until, by about the middle of September, he had added to the map some five hundred miles of newly discovered coast. Then winter set in, and the *Victory* was compelled to seek winter quarters, which were found in a bay afterwards named Felix Harbour. Convinced by this time of the uselessness of his steam engine, Ross threw it into the sea, and then turned his attention to the business of preparing every possible comfort for his crew during the long winter's imprisonment.

In the following spring, as soon as the weather permitted, Commander Ross started on a sledge journey with two Esquimaux guides, and discovered King William's Sound and King William's Land. Hopeful of making still further discoveries, he penetrated so far to the westward that at last he found himself two hundred miles from the ship and with only ten days' scanty rations between him and starvation. An immediate return was therefore imperative. He erected a high cairn of stones, in which he deposited a narrative of his proceedings, and then turned back, reaching his ship in an exhausted condition on June 13th.

After nearly a year's imprisonment the *Victory* once more found herself free, and on September 17th she proceeded again on her voyage of discovery. Her freedom was, however, short-lived, for on September 27th she was again in the grip of the ice ; and after a spell of liberty that had lasted only ten days her company found themselves faced with the prospect of another winter in the ice— and with the added trial of a reduced allowance of provisions.

During the following spring James Ross undertook several more sledge journeys ; and in the course of one of them he planted the British flag on the site of what he believed to be the Northern Magnetic Pole. It has since been proved that this is not, as Ross supposed, fixed to one spot, but moves from place to place within the glacial zone. The explorer's belief in his achievement was, however, sincere ; and his joy in it may best be judged from his own words. " As soon," he wrote, " as I had satisfied my own mind on the subject, I made known to the party this gratifying result of all our joint labours ; and it was then that, amidst mutual congratulations, we fixed the British flag on the spot, and took possession of the North Magnetic Pole and its adjoining territory in the name of Great Britain and King William IV. We had abundance of material for building in the fragments of limestone that covered the beach, and we therefore erected a cairn of some magnitude under which we buried a canister containing a record of the interesting fact, only regretting that we had not the means of constructing a pyramid of more importance, and of strength sufficient to withstand the assaults of time and of the Esquimaux. Had it been a pyramid as large as that of Cheops, I am not quite sure that it would have done more than satisfy our ambition under the feelings of that exciting day."

After a second imprisonment of eleven months, on August 28th, 1831, the crew of the *Victory* succeeded in warping the vessel out into the open sea ; but they were soon amongst the ice floes again ; and after a gallant struggle lasting a month, they found themselves, once more, on September 27th, completely frozen in. During their week of freedom the previous summer they had sailed three miles, and this time they had accomplished only four. At this rate the task of finally extricating the *Victory* from the icy barrier that shut her in seemed hopeless indeed, and at last, with that reluctance and heavy-heartedness with which the sailor always regards the last dread expedient, they decided to abandon her and make their way over the ice to Fury Beach, there to avail themselves of the boats, provisions and stores which would assist them in reaching Davis Straits.

So they set out, dragging their provisions and boats over the rough ice, and encountering terrific tempests of snow during the process. It took them a month of arduous labour to transport their stores from the ship to Fury Beach, but the work was finally finished, and then came the hardest task of all—that of bidding farewell to the *Victory*. " It was the first vessel," says her captain, " that I had ever been obliged to abandon, after having served in thirty-six, during a period of forty-two years. It was like the last parting with an old friend ; and I did not pass the point where she ceased to be visible without stopping to take a sketch of this melancholy desert, rendered more melancholy by the solitary, abandoned, helpless home of our past years, fixed in immovable ice, till Time should perform on her his usual work."

At Fury Beach they reared a cairn or hut, which they facetiously named Somerset House, and here they worked for a month to make their boats sea-worthy. At last all was ready, and these brave men, desperate but never quite despairing, set out on their perilous voyage. To their bitter disappointment they found that it was impossible to carry out their intention ; for Barrow's Strait, which they would have to negotiate, was an impenetrable mass of ice. There was, therefore, nothing for it but to return to Fury Beach and reconcile themselves to the dreary prospect of spending the winter there.

It was on October 7th that they got back to the beach. They built a huge wall of snow round " Somerset House," as an additional protection, and strengthened the roof of the house with spars, for the purpose of covering it also with snow ; and by this means, and with the aid of an extra stove, they made themselves tolerably comfortable until the increasing severity of the winter, added to the furious gales, made them absolute prisoners within the hut, and sorely tried their patience. To add to their trials, scurvy now began to attack them, and several of the party fell victims to the scourge, and their situation was becoming truly awful, since, if they were not liberated in the ensuing summer, little prospect appeared of their surviving another year. It was necessary to make a reduction in the allowance of preserved meats ; bread was somewhat deficient and the stock of wine and spirits was entirely exhausted. However, as they caught a few foxes, which were considered a delicacy, and there was plenty of flour, sugar, soups, and vegetables, a diet could be easily arranged sufficient to support the party.

As soon as the weather permitted, and while the ice still remained firm, the men busied themselves in transporting a stock of provisions to Batty Bay. The distance was not great—only thirty-two miles; but such were their difficulties owing to weakness through illness and the weight of the loads, that they had to go over the ground eight times, and the task occupied them a whole month.

On July 8th they abandoned Somerset House, and four days later they were established at Batty Bay, where they settled down to the anxious task of waiting for an opportunity for what they felt to be their final bid for liberty and life. For a month they watched and waited, and then, on August 15th, they ventured to embark. Making their way slowly among the masses of ice, with which the inlet was encumbered, they found to their great joy and relief that the wide expanse of Barrow's Strait was now open and navigable. Alternately rowing and sailing, they pushed on with renewed spirits, and passing Cape York, they found themselves on the night of the 25th in a good harbour on the eastern shore of Navy Board Inlet. On the following morning, at four o'clock, they were roused from their slumbers by the joyful intelligence of a ship being in sight, and never did men more hurriedly and energetically set out; but the elements conspired against them, and after a time the ship sailed away out of sight.

It was not long, however, before another vessel came into view. This was becalmed, and the men in the boats, literally rowing for their lives, soon came up with her. By a strange coincidence, she proved to be the very ship in which Ross had made his first voyage to the Arctic seas—the *Isabella*—now engaged in the whale fishery.

The men on the ship could scarcely believe the evidence of their own ears and eyes, when they found who the men in the boats really were ; and when they had been taken on board, Captain Ross had the doubtful pleasure of listening to a circumstantial account of his own death, which was believed in England to have taken place two years previously. Indeed, Ross had some difficulty in establishing his own identity ! But once it was proved that the gaunt, hollow-eyed leader of this forlorn group of men was verily the explorer who had so long since been given up for lost, the joy and enthusiasm of the men of the *Isabella* knew no bounds. They vied with each other in their offers of help and comfort for their fellow-countrymen, as it were given back from the dead. Captain Ross thus describes the scene :

" Though we had not been supported by our names and characters, we should not the less have claimed from charity the attentions that we received ; for never was seen a more miserable set of wretches. Unshaven since I know not when, dirty, dressed in the rags of wild beasts, and starved to the very bone, our gaunt and grim looks, when contrasted with the well-dressed and well-fed men around us, made us all feel (I believe for the first time) what we really were, as well as what we seemed to others. But the ludicrous soon took place of all other feelings ; in such a crowd, and in such confusion, all serious thought was impossible, while the new buoyancy of our spirits made us abundantly willing to be amused by the scenes which now opened. Every man was hungry, and was to be fed ; all were ragged, and were to be clothed ; there was not one to whom washing was not indispensable, nor one whom his beard did not deprive of all human semblance. All, everything, too, was to be done at once ; it was washing, shaving, dressing, eating, all intermingled ; it was all the materials of each jumbled together, while in the midst of all there were interminable questions to be asked and answered on both sides ; the adventures of the *Victory*, our own escape, the politics of England, and the news which was now four years old.

" But all subsided into peace at last. The sick were accommodated, the seamen disposed of, and all was done for us which care and kindness could perform.

"Night at length brought quiet and serious thoughts, and I trust there was not a man among us who did not then express, where it was due, his gratitude for that interposition which had raised us all from a despair which none could now forget, and had brought us from the very borders of a most distant grave to life and friends and civilization. Long accustomed, however, to a cold bed on the hard snow or the bare rock, few could sleep amid the comfort of our new accommodations. I was myself compelled to leave the bed which had been kindly assigned me, and take my abode in a chair for the night ; nor did it fare much better with the rest. It was for time to reconcile us to this sudden and violent change, to break through what had become habit, and inure us once more to the ways of our former days."

The home coming of the explorers was slightly delayed, as the *Isabella* remained some time longer in Baffin's Bay to prosecute the fishery, and so did not reach England until October 15th, 1833. The Arctic voyagers were regarded as men risen from the grave, and wherever they went they were followed by crowds of sympathizers. Honours fell thick and fast upon the brave leader of the expedition, and it was acknowledged on all hands that he had more than atoned for the mistakes of his first essay as an explorer. He was knighted, and Parliament made him a grant of five thousand pounds in consideration of his pecuniary outlay and privations.

The geographical gain of the expedition may not have been great ; but the personal bravery of the men who composed it is beyond question ; and the story of that long imprisonment amid the terrors of the far north, with all its accompaniments of privation and suffering so heroically borne, is worth remembrance for the lessons it conveys of patient, persistent effort and unceasing faith in the face of almost overwhelming difficulty and trial.

CHAPTER V.

A BRAVE MAN'S ENDEAVOUR.

THE long continued absence of Ross, as may be imagined, had roused many misgivings in the minds of his friends. As months lengthened into years, and as year succeeded year, hope gradually died in the hearts of most of them, and at last very few were left who believed there still remained any possibility of his being alive.

But these few were persistent, and when, at the end of four years, one of them—Captain Back—volunteered to lead a land expedition in search of Ross to the northern shore of America, his offer was accepted with grateful eagerness. Although the expedition of Captain Ross had not been undertaken under the auspices of the Government, his fate was felt to be a matter of national concern, and the Treasury contributed the sum of two thousand pounds towards the cost of the expedition, while four thousand pounds was raised for the purpose by public subscription. In order to help the gallant captain in his work the Colonial office gave him special authority, and the Hudson's Bay Company granted him a commission in their service, and promised him every assistance while in their territory in North America.

Everything being in order, Captain Back left Liverpool on February 17th, 1833, accompanied by Dr. Richard King as surgeon and naturalist, and he reached America after a stormy passage of thirty-five days. Thence he proceeded to Montreal, where he engaged the men necessary for the expedition ; and on June 28th, he began his journey. His crew comprised an Englishman, a man from Stornoway, two Canadians, two Metifs, or half-breeds, and three Iroquois Indians. "Babel itself," he says, "could not have produced a worse confusion of inharmonious sounds than was the conversation they kept up." In addition to these he had also obtained the services of Mr. A. R. McLeod, one of the servants of the Hudson's Bay Company.

At Fort Resolution, on Great Slave Lake, Back divided the members of his crew into two parts. Four of them he selected to accompany himself, and five he left with Mr. McLeod.

On August 19th, Back and his party began 'the ascent of Hoar Frost River, the crossing of which was a series of fearful cascades and rapids. Time after time they had to leave the water and drag their canoe through the woods of stunted firs that lined the banks—woods so thick, and so full of bogs and swamps that the whole party became disheartened, and but for their leader's determination and unfailing hopefulness would have turned back. But at last the difficulties were overcome and the ascent of this most troublesome river was safely accomplished. Captain Back was justifiably proud of his triumph, for he was the first traveller who had traced this turbulent stream to its source.

Winter was now approaching, and prudence demanded that they should return somewhat nearer to civilization. They found it impossible to travel back by the river, and, abandoning their canoe, they performed the journey on foot. Their course led them along a way that threatened death at almost every step—over precipitous rocks, and through frightful gorges and ravines; and only extreme caution preserved them from disaster.

On arriving at Fort Reliance the party found to their joy that Mr. McLeod had built up the frame-work of a winter residence for them. They set to work with a will to finish it, and it was very quickly ready for occupation. Not a day too soon, however, for winter, with all its attendant horrors in high latitudes, was upon them. Captain Back draws a vivid picture of the sufferings of the Indians at this time, owing to the scarcity of food. "Little or nothing," he says, "was to be gained by hunting, and the natives would stand around while our men were taking their meals, watching every mouthful with the most longing, imploring look, but yet never uttering a complaint. At other times they would, seated round the fire, occupy themselves in roasting and devouring small bits of their reindeer garments, which even when entire afforded them a very insufficient protection against a temperature of 102 degrees below freezing point. Famine with her gaunt and bony arm pursued them at every turn, withered their energies, and strewed them lifeless upon the cold bosom of the snow. Often did I share my own plate with the children, whose helpless state and piteous cries were peculiarly distressing. Compassion for the full-grown may or may not be felt, but that heart must be cased in steel which is insensible to the cry of a child for food."

When things were at their worst, Akaitcho, the chief of a friendly tribe with whom Captain Back had had dealings on a former expedition, brought a most welcome supply of meat, and many of the starving Indians, to Back's great relief, went away with him. The cold caused great suffering amongst the men; even the handling of their guns gave them such pain that they wrapped thongs of leather round the triggers to prevent their fingers from coming in contact with the steel. " On one occasion," says Back, " after washing my face within three feet of the fire my hair was actually clotted with ice before I had time to dry it."

Akaitcho continued to give most welcome help—indeed, it is doubtful whether without his assistance the party could have survived. " The great chief trusts us," he declared, " and it is better that ten Indians perish than that one white man should perish through our negligence and breach of faith."

When, towards the end of April, Captain Back began to prepare to renew his expedition, the welcome news arrived that Captain Ross had reached England in safety. Back thus describes the feelings of himself and his party when this joyful intelligence reached them : " In the fulness of our hearts we assembled together, and humbly offered up our thanks to that merciful Providence who, in the beautiful language of Scripture has said, ' Mine own will I bring again, as I did sometime from the deeps of the sea.' The thought of so wonderful a preservation for a time over- powered the common occurrences of life. We had just sat down to breakfast ; but our appetite was gone, and the day was passed in a feverish state of excitement."

Although the primary reason for his expedition was now no longer existent, Captain Back decided that instead of returning home, as he would have been quite justified in doing, he would continue his explorat on, turning his attention this time to the course of the Thlu-it-scho, or Great Fish River, which he desired to trace right down to the distant outlet where he believed it poured its waters into the Polar Sea.

Accordingly, on June 7th, all the necessary preparations having been completed, and McLeod having been previously sent on to hunt and deposit supplies of food at pre-arranged points on the route, Back set out with Mr. King, accompanied by four of his crew and an Indian guide. Before starting they buried the stores they were leaving behind and barricaded the house.

Back joined the remainder of his party at Artillery Lake, where they had been employed in preparing the boats. To the lightest and strongest of these, iron runners were attached, and it was then drawn over the frozen surface of the lake, by two men and six dogs. The men journeyed by night, and rested during the day ; but even so they found the glare of the snow very trying. The ice, too, was so bad that frequently the runners cut into it instead of gliding over it. Soon the weather .changed for the worse—hail, snow and rain alternating with sudden fierce squalls that threatened to overturn the boat. At last the pelting showers of sleet and snow so darkened the air and confused the travellers that it was only with the utmost difficulty they were able to keep their course.

After a fortnight's travel, during which they had had to fight almost every inch of their way, they came upon one of Mr. McLeod's food depôts. This meant literally new life for the exhausted men, and though part of the food consisted of musk ox flesh, unpleasantly impregnated with the odour from which it takes its name, the men took it thankfully.

At the end of June the Great Fish River was reached, and here Captain Back called a halt to review his position, and take stock. He calculated that the task he had set himself would occupy about three months ; and after careful thought he concluded he had a sufficient food supply for that period ; but the task that faced him was great enough to deter any but the stoutest heart. The total weight of stores and outfit was about five thousand pounds ; and the difficulty of transporting this over ice and rocks, by a circuitous route of two hundred miles or more can hardly be imagined. And the work was rendered the more arduous by the fact that in some places the ice formed innumerable spikes that pierced the feet like needles, while in other parts it was so black and decayed that it threatened at every step to engulf the traveller.

In a day or two the party caught up with

McLeod, who was then sent back, with ten men and fourteen dogs, his instructions being to proceed to Fort Resolution and there await certain stores promised by the Hudson's Bay Company ; to build a house in some suitable spot to serve as a permanent fishing station, and to return to the banks of the Great Fish River by the middle of September, in readiness to afford Back and his party any help they might require.

Faithful old Akaitcho, hearing of Captain Back's intention of exploring the river, hastened to warn him of the dangers of his enterprise. " I have known the chief a long time," he said, " and I am afraid I shall never see him again. I will go to him." He accordingly went after the explorer, and on meeting him warned him of the dangers of a river of which, he declared, no living Indian had any knowledge. He cautioned him, too, against the Esquimaux, declaring that under the guise of friendship they hid much treachery. " I am afraid," he added, " that I shall never see you again ; but should you escape from the great water, take care that you are not caught by the winter, and thrown into a situation like that in which you were before ; for you are alone, and the Indians cannot assist you."

The good old chief's touching solicitude was greatly appreciated ; but Captain Back's mind was made up. He had counted the cost before ever he started, and he intended to carry out his project. Some of the men who were no longer required were dismissed, and sent to rejoin McLeod, and with a crew of ten the captain began his journey down the great unknown river.

The weight of cargo in the boat was between three and four thousand pounds, exclusive of the awning, poles, sails, etc., and the crew— a sufficiently heavy load for a light craft to bear down a stream never before explored by man.

Possibly if the leader of the party had known what awaited him he would never have ventured ; for the river proved to be one long succession of falls, rapids and cataracts. Time after time the men held their breath, expecting nothing but that their frail, leaky craft would be dashed to pieces, as it shot over some rapid towards the foam-covered rocks below. How the boat lived was a mystery to them all. On one occasion when they struck a rock, the boat was only saved by every man jumping out into the breakers and keeping her stern up the stream till she was cleared ; and they had hardly time to scramble back to their places before they were carried with tremendous force past a stream which joined from the westward.

Within a length of three miles they successfully negotiated five rapids, each with its own dangerous features ; and then another

came into view, appalling in its length, full
of rocks, and boulders, its sides hemmed in
by walls of ice, and its current flying with
terrific velocity.   The boat was lightened
of her cargo, and Captain Back placed himself
on a high rock, with an anxious desire to see
her run the rapid.   He had every hope which
confidence in the dexterity and judgment of
his men could inspire, but it was impossible
not to feel that one crash would be fatal
to the expedition.   Away they went with the
speed of an arrow, and in a moment the foam
and rocks hid them from view.   Back at
last heard what sounded in his ear like a
wild shriek, and he saw Dr. King, who was
a hundred yards before him, make a sign
with his gun and then run forward.   Back
followed with an agitation which may be
easily imagined, when to his inexpressible
joy he found that the shriek was the trium-
phant whoop of the crew, who had landed
safely in a small bay below.   And this was
only one incident typical of many which befel
these fearless men in their course of a hundred
miles along a river abounding in frightful
whirlpools and rapids.

In the course of the journey Back had an
unpleasant reminder that the native Indian
is not always a man of unimpeachable honour.
On opening one of the bags of pemmican it
was found that some pilfering redskins had
ingeniously removed the original contents

of the bag, and artfully substituted successive layers of mixed sand, stones, and green meat. The discovery was disconcerting, for the men naturally feared that the other bags had been similarly tampered with ; but on examination it was found that they were all intact, and moreover that the pemmican they contained was sound and well tasted.

The course of the river was not uniformly northward ; and at one point it took such a decided turn to the south that Captain Back feared it did not find its outlet in the Polar Sea after all ; but the southern tendency proved to his great joy to be only temporary.

At the end of July the party met a tribe of about thirty-five Esquimaux. Remembering the warning of Akaitcho, Captain Back was somewhat dubious about approaching them ; but their unaffected friendliness quickly disarmed him, and they proved most helpful— assisting in the transport of the boat over a long and difficult portage to which the crew were quite unequal. Captain Back generously acknowledged that but for the timely help of these friendly folk it was doubtful whether he would have been able to reach the sea at all.

They were now close to the mouth of the river ; and while threading their course between some sandbanks with a strong current, they caught sight of a majestic headland in the extreme distance to the

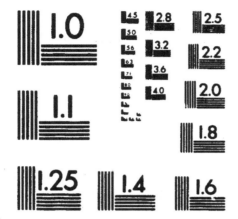

MICROCOPY RESOLUTION TEST CHART
NATIONAL BUREAU OF STANDARDS
STANDARD REFERENCE MATERIAL 1010a
(ANSI and ISO TEST CHART No 2)

north, which had a coast-like appearance. This important promontory Back subsequently named after our gracious Queen of glorious memory—" Victoria."

" This, then," observes the explorer, " may be considered as the mouth of the Thlu-it-scho, which after a violent and tortuous course of five hundred and thirty geographical miles, running through an iron-ribbed country, without a single tree on the whole line of its banks, expanding into five large lakes, with clear horizon, most embarrassing to the navigator, and broken into falls, cascades and rapids to the number of eighty-three in the whole, pours its waters at last into the Polar Sea."

Along the eastern shore of the river mouth Back made slow progress for several days, his course greatly impeded by a solid body of drift-ice. For ten days he persevered in his efforts to explore this bleak, inhospitable shore, under conditions which at last seriously dispirited the brave men who accompanied him. The weather was wet, chilly and foggy ; and the only vegetation a species of moss and fern so wet that it would not burn. During all these days they were therefore without fuel—a highly dangerous predicament in a place of such extreme cold. " Almost without water, without any means of warmth, or any kind of warm or comforting food, sinking knee-deep as they proceeded on land in the soft slush and snow, no wonder that some of the best men, benumbed in their limbs, and dispirited by the dreary and unpromising prospect before them, broke out for a moment in low murmurings that theirs was a hard and painful duty."

Loth though he was to turn back, the captain was forced to the conclusion that it was impossible to proceed. Three of his best walkers volunteered for a land expedition and a final effort ; but, after travelling only fifteen miles, heavy rain and the swampy nature of the ground compelled them to give up the attempt. When they came and reported their failure Captain Back resolved to return. " Reflecting," he says, " on the long and dangerous stream we had to ascend, combining all the bad features of the worst rivers in the country, the hazard of the falls and the rapids, and the slender hope which remained of our attaining a single mile further, I felt I had no choice." He therefore gathered his men round him, and unfurling the British flag, which was saluted with three cheers, he announced his determination. On hearing this, the men, whose health had suffered severely through lack of warmth and suitable food, set to work with a will to prepare for the return journey. They battled cheerfully with the difficulties of the way, which were doubled when they found themselves once more between the banks of the river, as they had to proceed against the stream. All the obstacles of rocks, rapids, sand-banks, and long portages had to be faced, but they worked and struggled without a murmur. Even the fact that many of the deposits of provisions which they had relied upon for the needs of the homeward journey had been discovered and destroyed by wolves did not daunt them.

By mid-September they met McLeod and his party who, faithful to their instructions, were waiting for them at Sand Hill Bay.

A few days later their progress was interrupted by a most formidable fall, almost perpendicular ; and as they found it impossible to convey the boat further by land owing to the rough and mountainous nature of the country, most of the declivities being covered with thin ice and the whole hidden by snow, they abandoned it, and continued their journey on foot, each man carrying a pack weighing about seventy-five pounds.

Towards the end of September they arrived safely at their old quarters at Fort Reliance, after an absence of nearly four months. Spent with toil they were, and weary, but " truly grateful for the manifold mercies they had experienced in the course of their long and perilous journey." They made the best arrangements they could for their comfort during the winter that was before

them ; and as it was obvious that the provisions in store would not suffice to sustain
the whole party, all except six went with
McLeod to the fisheries. The Indians proved
friendly and helpful, and the winter passed
not unpleasantly.

As soon as winter was over Captain Back
made arrangements to return to England.
After calling at the Fisheries to bid farewell
to his friend McLeod, he proceeded to New
York, and embarked for England, where he
arrived on September 8th, after an absence of
two years and a half, Dr. King following
him a month later.

Captain Back was honoured with an
audience of the King, who expressed approval
of his efforts, first in the cause of humanity,
and next in that of geographical and scientific
research. The Captain was afterwards
knighted in 1835, and the Royal Geographical
Society awarded him their gold medal in
recognition of his discovery of the Great Fish
River, and navigating it to the sea on the
Arctic coast.

It has been justly said that it is " impossible
to read the record of Captain Back's exploration without being struck with astonishment
at the extent of suffering which the human
frame can endure, and at the same time the
wondrous display of fortitude which was
exhibited under circumstances of such unusual peril as to invest the narrative with the

character of romantic fiction, rather than an unexaggerated tale of actual reality." He certainly proved himself a man of rare courage and wonderful resource, and he deserves the place he has gained amongst those whose bravery renders them conspicuous in their country's history.

CHAPTER VI.

A FIGHT WITH THE ICE FLOES.

CAPTAIN BACK'S expedition of 1833 had established his reputation as a fearless explorer; and when, three years later, another venture to the polar regions was organized, it was generally recognized that he was the most fitting man to command it. The main object of this expedition was survey; but, geographically considered, it was a failure. It supplies, however, some wonderful instances of the daring of British sailors, and of their bravery under circumstances of extreme peril.

Captain Back left England on June 14th, 1836 in the *Terror*, with instructions to sail to Repulse or Wagner Bay, and thence take a party overland to the eastern shore of Prince Regent Islet.

Six weeks after leaving England Back crossed Davis Straits, where he sighted an enormous iceberg, " the perpendicular face of which was not less than three hundred feet high." This great ice mountain was the grim forerunner of many others ; and shortly afterwards the vessel was in the midst of ice floes, amongst which she soon became fast locked, remaining practically immovable for nine months.

On September 5th the weather suddenly changed, and every man on the ship hurried oft to the nearest open water, armed with axes, ice chisels, handspikes and long poles, to do battle with the ice and try to make a clear passage for their imprisoned vessel. The work was arduous and difficult, and often enough a man, when hauling a big mass of ice out of the way, would slip and fall into the water up to his neck. Such an experience was not pleasant in an Arctic temperature, but it was met with a laugh and a joke, in which the drenched sailor would join with the rest.

But the brave efforts of the men were only partly successful, and soon again the ice triumphed and gripped the ship as tightly as before. On September 20th a breeze sprang up, and set the huge masses of ice in motion again ; and the pounding and crashing of the great floes, as hard as rocks, against the sides of the ship, threatened destruction at almost any moment. The greatest danger occurred when an enormous floe-piece split in two "and the extreme violence of the pressure curled and crumbled up the windward ice in an awful manner, forcing it against the beam fully eighteen feet high. The ship creaked as it were in agony; and strong as she was, must have been stove and crushed had not some of the smaller masses been forced under her bottom, and so diminished the strain by actually lift ng her bow nearly two feet out of the water.

"In this perilous crisis steps were taken to have e·· ··ng in readiness for hoisting out the b: ⸱ ⸱. without creating unnecessary alarm ·· · rs and men were called on the quartei ⸱⸱:, and desired, in case of emergency, to be active in the performance of their duties at the respective stations then notified to them. It was a serious moment for all, as the pressure still continued, nor could we expect much, if any, abatement until the wind changed.

"At noon the weather and our prospects remained the same. The barometer was falling, and the temperature was twenty-six degrees, with unceasing snow. Much ice had been sunk under her bottom, and a doubt existed whether it was not finding its way beneath the lee floe also; for the uplifted ruins, within fifty paces of the weather beam, were advancing slowly towards us, like an immense wave fraught with destruction. Resistance would not, could not, have been effectual beyond ⸱ few seconds, for what of human construction could withstand the impact of an icy continent driven onward by a furious storm ?

" In the meantime symptoms, too un-equivocal to be misunderstood, demonstrated the intensity of the pressure. The butt ends began to start, and the copper in which the galley apparatus was fixed became creased, sliding doors refused to shut, and leaks found access through the bolt heads and bulls' eyes. On sounding the well, too, an increase of water was reported, not sufficient to excite apprehension in itself, but such as to render hourly pumping necessary. Moved by these indications, and to guard against the worst, I ordered the provisions and preserved meats, with various other necessaries, to be got up from below and stored on deck, so as to be ready at a moment to be thrown upon the large floe alongside.   To add to our anxiety night closed prematurely, when suddenly, from some unknown cause, in which, if we may so deem without presumption, the finger of Providence was manifest, the floe which threatened instant destruction turned so as in a degree to protect us against an increase of pressure, though for several hours after the same creaking and grinding sounds continued to annoy our ears. The barometer and the other instruments fell with a regularity unprecedented, for the gale was broken and by midnight it had abated considerably."

The worst of the danger was now over, and

on the following day Back records that " there was a lateral motion in some pieces of the surrounding ice, and, after several astounding thumps under water against the bottom, the ship, which had been lifted high beyond the line of flotation, and thrown somewhat over to port, suddenly started up and almost righted. Still, however, she inclined more than was agreeable to port, nor was it until one mass of ponderous dimensions burst from its imprisonment below, that she altogether regained her upright position. On beholding the walls of ice on either side between which she had been nipped, I was astonished at the tremendous force she had sustained."

The shape of the vessel was actually stamped upon the ice as in a die ; and the fact that the *Terror* ha· sustained no serious damage through the tremendous grip of the ice was a splendid testimony to the genius and the workmanship of those who had fitted her for her task. Amongst the sailors on board were many old Greenland seamen, and they declared they had never seen any other ship that could have withstood such a pressure. Beyond the fresh caulking of the seams on deck there was nothing for the carpenters to do in the way of repairs ; and when the well was sounded it was found the *Terror* was still sound and without a leak.

Then suddenly, when the ship had been fast in the ice for a month, the pressure again relaxed, and the solid ice broke up into tremendous fragments which came grinding and pounding against the vessel's sides. It was impossible, however, for her to get free ; and the only result of the commotion was to raise her stern seven-and-a-haif feet above the proper level, and to correspondingly depress her bow, the result being that the deck was an inclined plane, difficult and dangerous to walk upon.

In the beginning of October the ship had practically recovered her normal position, and the men found employment in building snow-walls round her, and in erecting an observatory on the floe. Like many another Arctic explorer before and since his day, Back found it necessary to organize amusements for his men, and in various ways he managed to provide a good deal of pleasure for them. On the whole they seem to have been a somewhat difficult crew to manage. They had been hastily gathered together, Back says, " and for the most part were composed of people who had never before been out of a collier. Some half dozen, indeed, had served in Greenland vessels, but the laxity which is there permitted rendered them little better than the former. A few men-of-war's men who were also on board were worth the wh 'e lot put together. The want of discipline and of attention to personal comfort was most conspicuous ; and though the wholesome regulations practised in Her Majesty's service were most rigidly attended to in the *Terror*, yet such was the unsociability, though without any ill-will, that it was only by a steady and undeviating system pursued by the first lieutenant that they were brought at all together with the feeling of messmates. At first, though nominally at the same mess, and eating at the same table, many of them would secrete their allowance, with other unmanly and unsailor-like practices. This was another proof added to the many I had already witnessed, how greatly discipline improves the mind and manners, and how much the regular service men are to be preferred for all hazardous or difficult enterprizes. Reciprocity of kindness, a generous and self-denying disposition, a spirit of frankness, a hearty and above-board manner—these are the true characteristics of the British seaman, and the want of these is seldom compensated by other qualities.

"In our case, and I mention this merely to show the difference of older and modern times, there were only three or four in the ship who could not write. All read, some recited whole pages of poetry, others sang French songs. Yet, with all this, had they been left to themselves, I verily believe a more unsociable, suspicious and uncomfortable

set of people could not have been found.
Oh, if the two are incompatible, give me
the old Jack Tar, who would stand out for
his ship and give his life for his messmates."

The dreary Arctic winter of one long, unbroken night passed slowly, though not
without excitement when occasionally the
ice began to move. But it was not until
February 20th that this peril of moving ice
seriously menaced them. On that day, for
three hours after midnight, the walls of their
icy prison moved backwards and forwards,
threatening to crush the vessel at any moment.
So serious was the danger that after eight
o'clock in the morning, in an interval of
comparative calm, Back addressed the crew,
" reminding them," he says, " that as
Christians and British seamen they were
called upon to conduct themselves with coolness and fortitude, and that, independently
of the obligations imposed by the Articles
of War, every one ought to be influenced by
the still higher motive of a conscientious
desire to perform his duty. I gave them to
understand that I expected from one and all,
in the event of any disaster, an implicit
obedience to and energetic execution of every
order that they might receive from the officers,
as well as kind and compassionate help to the
sick. On their observance of these injunc-
tions, I warned them, our ultimate safety
might depend. Some fresh articles of warm

CAPTAIN BACK ADDRESSING HIS BRAVE SEAMEN.

clothing were then dealt out to them; and
as the moment of destruction was uncertain,
I desired that the small bags in which
those things were contained should be placed
on deck with the provisions, so as to be ready
at an instant. The forenoon was spent in
getting up bales of blankets, bear-skins,
provisions, and, in short, whatever might be
necessary if the ship should be suddenly
broken up; and spars were rigged over the
quarters to hoist them out. Meanwhile the
ice moved but little, though the hour of full
moon was passed; but at noon it began to
drift slowly to the northward. We were
now from five to eight miles off the nearest
land.

"Though I had seen vast bodies of ice from
Spitzbergen to 150 degrees west longitude
under various aspects, some beautiful, and all
more or less awe-inspiring, I had never witnessed, nor even imagined, anything so fearfully
magnificent as the moving towers and ram-
parts that now frowned on every side. Had
the still extensive pieces of which the floe was
formed split and divided like those further
off, the effect would have been far less in-
jurious to the ship; but though cracked and
rent, the parts from some inexplicable cause
closed again for a time and drove with
accelerated and almost resistless force against
the defenceless vessel. In the forenoon the
other boats were hoisted higher up, to save

them from damage in the event of the ship being thrown much on her broadside.

" For three hours we remained unmolested, though the ice outside of the floe was moving in various directions, some pieces almost whirling round, and of course in the effort disturbing others. At 5 .m., however, the piece near the ship having previously opened enough to allow of her resuming a nearly upright position, collapsed again with a force that made every plank complain ; and further pressure being added at six o'clock, an ominous cracking was heard that only ceased on her being lifted bodily up eighteen inches. The same unwelcome visitation was repeated an hour afterwards, in consequence of the closing of a narrow lane directly astern.

" The night was very fine, but the vapour which arose from the many cracks, as well as from the small open space alongside, quickly becoming converted into small spiculæ of snow, rendered the cold intolerably keen to those who faced the wind. Up to midnight we were not much annoyed, and for four hours afterwards, on February 21st, all was quiet. Every man had gone to rest with his clothes on and was agreeably surprised at being so long undisturbed by the usual admonitory grinding. However, at 4 a.m. a commotion was heard, which appeared to be confined to the angle contained between north and north-west. On looking

round at daybreak it was found that the
ship had been released by the retreating of the
ice, and had nearly righted ; but at 5 a.m.
she rose eighteen inches as before. She was
then at intervals jerked up from the pressure
underneath, with a groan each time from the
woodwork."

Day after day the danger continued. The
men on the *Terror* were helpless, but never
hopeless, though they knew that death
menaced them all the while. All they could
do was to see to every possible strengthening
of their ship, and keep themselves prepared
for the catastrophe that seemed inevitable.
On March 15th the conditions changed
again for the worse, and the *Terror* was put to
a severer test of endurance than any she had
yet encountered. Back describes it in the
following thrilling narrative :

" While we were gliding quickly along the
land—which, I may here remark, had become
more broken and rocky, though without
obtaining an altitude of more than perhaps
one or two hundred feet—at 1.45 p.m., without
the least warning, a heavy rush came upon the
ship ; and, with a tremendous pressure on
the larboard quarter, bore her over upon the
heavy mass upon her starboard quarter.
The strain was severe in every part, though
from the forecastle she appeared to be
moving in the easier manner toward the
land-ice.

"Suddenly, however, a loud crack was heard below the mainmast as if the keel were broken or carried away ; and simultaneously the outer sternpost from the ten feet mark was split down to an unknown extent and projected to the larboard side upwards of three feet. The ship was thrown up by the stern to the seven-and-a-half feet mark ; and that damage had been done was soon placed beyond doubt by the increase of leakage, which now amounted to three feet per hour. Extra pumps were worked, and while some of the carpenters were fixing diagonal shores forward, others were examining the orlops and other parts. It was reported to me by the first lieutenant, master, and carpenter, that nothing could be detected inside, though apprehensions were entertained by the two former that some serious injury had been inflicted.

"In spite of the commotion the different pieces of our floe still remained firm ; but, being unable to foresee what might take place during the night, I ordered the cutters and two whale boats to be lowered down, and hauled with their stores to places considered more secure. This was accordingly done, though not under two hours and a half, even with the advantage of daylight. The ship was still setting fast along shore, and much too close to the fixed ice ; but it was not until past 8 p.m. that any suspicious movement

was noticed near us ; then, however, a continually increasing rush was heard, which
at 10.45 p.m. came on with a heavy roar
towards the larboard quarter, upturning in
its progress, and rolling onward with it an
immense wall of ice. This advanced so fast
that though all hands were immediately
called, they had barely time, with the greatest
exertion, to extricate three of the boats, one
of them, in fact, being hoisted up when only
a few feet from the crest of the solid wave
which held a steady course directly for the
quarter, almost overtopping it, and continuing to elevate itself until about twenty-
five feet high. A piece had just reached the
rudder, flung athwart the stern, and at the
moment when, to all appearances, both that
and a portion at least of the framework were
expected to be staved in and buried beneath
the ruins, the motion ceased ; at the same
time the crest of the nearest part of the wave
toppled over, leaving a deep wall extending
from thence beyond the quarter. The effect
of the whole was a leak in the extreme run,
oozing, as far as could be ascertained, from
somewhere about the stern post. It ran in
along the lining like a rill for about half an
hour, when it stopped, probably closed by a
counter pressure. The other leaks could be
kept under by the incessant use of one pump.

" Our intervals of repose were now very
short, for at 12.50 a.m., March 16th, another

rush drove irresistibly on the larboard quarter and stern, and, forcing the ship ahead, raised her upon the ice. A chaotic ruin followed; our poor and cherished courtyard, its walls and arched doors, gallery, and well trodden paths, were rent, and in some parts ploughed up like dust. The ship was careened fully four streaks, and sprang a leak as before. Scarcely were ten minutes left us for the expression of our astonishment that anything of human build could outli·'e such assaults, when at 1 a.m. another equally violent rush succeeded, and, in its way towards the starboard quarter, threw up a rolling wave thirty feet high, crowned by a blue, square mass of many tons, resembling the entire side of a house, which, after hanging for some time in doubtful poise on the ridge, at length fell with a crash into the hollow, in which, as in a cavern, the after-part of the ship seemed imbedded.

" It was, indeed, an awful crisis, rendered more frightful from the mistiness of the night, and dimness of the moon. The poor ship cracked and trembled violently, and no one could say that the next minute would not be her last, and, indeed, his own, too; for with her our means of safety would probably perish.

" The leak continued, and again (most likely, as before, from counter pressure) the principal one closed up. When all this was over, and there seemed to be a chance of respite, I ordered a double allowance of preserved meat, etc., to be issued to the crew, whose long exposure to the cold rendered some extra stimulant necessary.   Until 4 a.m. the rushes still kept coming from different directions, but fortunately with diminished force.   From that hour to 8 a.m. everything was still, and the ice quite stationary, somewhat to the westward of the singular point, terminating as it were in a knob, which was the farthest eastern extreme yesterday.   We certainly were not more than three miles from the barren and irregular land abeam, which received the name of Point Terror.   To this was attached a rugged shelf of what, for the time, might be called shore ice, having at its seaward face a mural ridge of unequal, though in many parts imposing, height, certainly not less than from fifty to sixty feet."

After this terrifying experience, the conditions somewhat improved, and the crew of the *Terror* looked forward with fresh hope to release from their icy prison.   Their hope was justified `eventually ; but before relief came their ship had been for nine months enclosed in the ice, with which it drifted several hundreds of miles.   On July 11th the crew were engaged upon their customary labour when, as they drew near the sternpost, various noises and crackings beneath them plainly hinted that something more than usual was in progress. "After breakfast," writes Back, "I visited them, and scarcely had I taken a few turns on deck and descended to my cabin when a loud rumbling notified that the ship had broken her icy bonds, and was sliding gently down into her own element. I ran instantly on deck, and joined in the cheers of the officers and men, who, dispersed on different pieces of ice, took this significant method of expressing their feelings.

"It was a sight not to be forgotten. Standing on the taffrail, I saw the dark, bubbling water below, and enormous masses of ice gently vibrating and springing to the surface ; the first lieutenant was just climbing over the stern, while other groups were standing apart, separated by this new gulf ; and the spars, together with working implements, were resting half in the water, half on the ice, while the saw, the instrument whereby this sudden effect had been produced, was bent double, and in that position forcibly detained by the body it had severed."

The crew had actually cut through the ice to within four feet of the stern-post when the disruption took place, and had ceased work for a few moments. They had only just time to clamber on board into safety.

Covered with honourable scars of wounds received in her tremendous nine months battle with the ice, but still seaworthy, the

Terror finally shook herself free of the floes that had vainly tried to conquer her, and on July 4th set sail for home. England was reached in due course without mishap of any kind; and the *Terror* reached port safely, with a story of perilous adventure such as is almost without parallel in that most dangerous of naval enterprises, the sailing of the polar seas.

CHAPTER VII.

THE STORY OF SIR JOHN FRANKLIN.

PRE-EMINENT in the long list of Britain's naval heroes stands the name of Sir John Franklin. Born at Spilsby, in Lincolnshire, he was destined by his father for the Church. But from the day when, as a schoolboy at Louth, he caught his first glimpse of the sea, he resolved that he would be a sailor.

Thinking that a little actual experience of the hardships of a sailor's life would most probably cure the boy of what his father regarded as mere youthful folly, he was permitted a trial trip in a merchantman to Lisbon. This taste of life afloat, however, only confirmed him in his determination ; and realizing that further opposition was useless, his father allowed him to join the navy in 1800. His first long voyage was to Australia ; and on the return journey his ship was wrecked on a coral reef where, with ninety-three fellow voyagers, he remained for fifty days on a narrow sandbank only four feet above the level of the water. On his return to England he joined the *Bellerophon*, and saw service at the battle of Trafalgar as a signal midshipman. His promotion was rapid, and he had before him the prospect of a brilliant naval career if he had chosen to follow the usual line of his profession. But he had long cherished the ambition to make a name for himself as an Arctic explorer; and when in 1819 an opportunity presented itself of venturing as far as the Polar Sea, he eagerly seized it.

Associated with Franklin in this his first expedition to the far north were Dr. Richardson, Back, Hood, and a sailor named Hepburn. The party left England on May 22nd, 1819, and three months later they reached York Factory, Hudson's Bay. During the winter that followed they journeyed 857 miles to Chipewyan; and in the succeeding sp..ng reached Fort Providence. Thence they made their way to Winter Lake where they built a house, which they named Fort Enterprise, in which they spent the winter. Between this house and Fort Providence Back and some of the others made many journeys, travelling in all 1,104 miles in bitter weather, to bring up supplies for the next summer's travel.

At the end of June, 1821, the Coppermine River was reached, and eighteen days later the travellers arrived at the sea coast. They were now 317 miles from their last winter quarters; and for more than a third of this distance they hauled their canoe and baggage over snow and ice. At Chipewyan Franklin had engaged a number of native Canadians to join his party, and these men, though eager as children for the excitement and novelty of their new experiences under Franklin's leadership, became alarmed when they learned that the next of his daring proposals was a journey eastward of 550 miles through an icy sea, on which they had to embark in their frail canoes, with only fifteen days' provisions on board. However, it was impossible to turn back; so with many misgivings they started. But from the outset the voyagers were beset with difficulties. Fierce storms arose, which badly damaged their canoes and spoilt much of their store of food, and at last, when it became evident that to persist in his endeavour was only to court death for the men whose lives were in his care, Franklin changed his plans and decided to steer westward for Arctic Sound, and attempt to reach his old quarters at Fort Enterprise by way of Hood's River.

After an adventurous voyage, in the course of which they were more than once almost at the point of starvation through the failure of their hunters to secure fresh supplies of food, the party reached Hood's River on August 26th; " and here," says Franklin, " terminated our voyage on the Arctic Sea, during which we had gone over 650 geographical miles. Our Canadian voyagers could not restrain their joy at having turned their backs on the sea, and they spent the evening in talking over their past adventures with much humour and no little exaggeration. It is due to their character to mention that they displayed much courage in encountering the dangers of the sea, magnified to them by their novelty."

From the remnants of their old and now useless canoes the travellers constructed two smaller ones, and on September 1st they started in a direct line for Point Lake, 149 miles distant. They had, however, only proceeded about a dozen miles when they were overtaken by a terrible snow storm which raged with such fury that for a week they were obliged to remain in camp muffled up in blankets and skins. For Franklin and all the poor fellows who were with him this was in truth a deadly delay; for while they remained imprisoned in their cheerless, cold camp they were consuming the food that should have served them to the end of their journey; and before the storm was over the last piece of pemmican had been served out. They were all terribly weakened, owing to severe privation, when, the storm having at last abated, they attempted to proceed; and Franklin himself was seized with a fainting fit, due to sudden exposure and exhaustion.

The only food they had remaining was a little portable soup ; and this—their last meal— they cooked over a fire made from the fragments of one of the canoes which had been crushed in a fall.

For two days the only sustenance of these much tried men was a lichen named by the Canadians *tripe de roche*. After this, however, they had the good fortune to kill a large musk ox, which, although the flesh is extremely unpalatable, they ate thankfully. Then supplies again failed ; and the men, hopeless and despondent, gave up in despair and abandoned their second canoe, leaving behind also their fishing nets and many articles of value to the expedition. But in this extremity, as so often happens, an example of superb heroism and unselfishness served to cheer the leader and his brother officers. They were gathered round a small fire, enduring the tortures of extreme hunger, when one of the Canadians, Perrault, approached, and generously offered to each of them a piece of pemmican which, with much self-denial, he had saved from his own small daily allowance. "It was received," said Franklin, in relating the incident, "with great thankfulness, and such an instance of self-denial and kindness filled our eyes with tears."

The travellers had now reached a branch of the Coppermine River, which it was necessary for them to cross ; and the most reckless

PERRAULT OFFERING FOOD TO HIS STARVING COMRADES.

amongst them realized now their folly in having abandoned the canoe in which they might so easily have made the crossing. Still, nothing was to be gained by wasting time in vain regrets, so the whole party set to work to make a raft of willows. The task was not an easy one, and it occupied them some days; and when at last the raft was completed they found it impossible to get it across the stream.

"In this hopeless condition," says Franklin, "with certain starvation staring them in the face, Dr. Richardson, actuated by the noble desire of making a last effort for the safety of the party, and of relieving his suffering companions from a state of misery which could only terminate, and that speedily, in death, volunteered to make the attempt to swim across the stream, carrying with him a line by which the raft might be hauled over.

"He launched into the stream with the line round his m⋮ ᵗᵉ, but when he had got to a short dista rom the opposite bank, his arms became ⸱ᵤᵤumed wiⁱⁱ cold, and he lost the power of moving them. Still he persevered, and, turning on his back, had nearly gained the opposite shore when his legs also became powerless, and to our infinite alarm we beheld him sink. We instantly hauled upon the line, and he came again on the surface, and was gradually drawn ashore in

an almost lifeless state. Being rolled up in
blankets he was placed before a good fire
of willows, and fortunately was just able to
speak sufficiently to give some slight directions
respecting the manner of treating him. He
recovered strength gradually, and through
the blessing of God was enabled in the course
of a few hours to converse, and by the evening
was sufficiently recovered to remove into the
tent. We then regretted to learn that the
skin of his whole left side was deprived of
feeling in consequence of exposure to too great
heat. He did not perfectly recover the
sensation of that side until the following
summer. I cannot describe what everyone
felt at beholding the skeleton which the
doctor's debilitated frame exhibited when he
stripped. I shall best explain his state and
that of the party by the following extract
from his journal :

" 'It may be worthy of remark that I should
have had little hesitation in any former period
of my life at plunging into water even below
38 degrees Fahrenheit ; but at this time I was
reduced almost to skin and bone, and, like
the rest of the party, suffered from degrees of
cold that would have been disregarded in
health and vigour. During the whole of
our march we experienced that no quantity
of clothing would keep us warm while we
fasted ; but on those occasions on which we
were enabled to go to bed with full stomachs

we passed the night in a warm and comfortable manner.'

" In following the details of our friend's narrow escape," adds Franklin, " I have omitted to mention that when he was about to step into the water, he put his foot on a dagger, which cut him to the bone ; but this misfortune could not stop him from attempting the execution of his generous undertaking."

The difficulty of crossing the river was at length overcome, but even then there remained a great deal of arduous travel before safety could be reached. How arduous may be gathered from the fact that one day Franklin spent three hours in a vain attempt to wade through the snow to one of his men who was only three quarters of a mile away. The leaders of the expedition were indeed in a pitiable plight. Richardson was lame, as well as exhausted by privation ; Back could only hobble along with the aid of a stick, and Hood was so reduced by starvation that he was little more than a living skeleton. Yet the courage of these men never wavered. However weak the flesh, the spirit never faltered, and they kept on, with dogged determination, and with unfailing faith in their leader. Hepburn, too, although suffering as much as the others, was consistently cheerful and hopeful, and he proved indefatigable in collecting the *tripe de roche* which was now their staple food.

With winter almost upon them the men realized that their one chance of life lay in reaching shelter speedily. Franklin therefore decided to push forward, with eight of the men, hoping to be able to send back assistance to the others. Four of the eight, however, broke down shortly after a start was made, and turned back. Only one of them reached the camp; the other three were never heard of again. When Franklin arrived at Fort Enterprise a crushing disappointment awaited him, for he found the place deserted. The silence of desolation was there, and not a scrap of food could the starving men discover. It was something, however, to have gained shelter; and by boiling bones and pieces of skin they managed to obtain a little sustenance which was an improvement on the portions of their boots which they had eaten during the journey.

After a brief halt Franklin valiantly attempted to reach the next fort; but finding that he had travelled only four miles in six hours he was compelled to give up the effort, and returned to the house, sending two of the Canadians on. Eighteen days went by, and then Dr. Richardson arrived, with Hepburn. Hood had been shot by one of their Indian followers. Near Fort Enterprise Hepburn had shot a partridge, and a sixth part of this was the first morsel of flesh Franklin and his three companions had tasted for thirty-one days.

And now, when they were in the very last extremity of hunger and weakness, help arrived. Back, who had been sent forward with some of the others many days previously, had reached Fort Enterprise before it was deserted. He had been obliged to go on with the others when the fort was abandoned, but he had sent back three Indians with welcome relief. After the food and rest they so sorely needed the whole party set out again, and succeeded in reaching Fort York with comparatively little difficulty. From thence the way was easy, and eventually Franklin and his brave companions, with the exception of poor Hood, whose life had been forfeit to an Indian's treachery, reached England in safety, after one of the most thrilling and dangerous journeys ever recorded.

After such an experience Franklin might well have resolved that he would never venture again into the perilous regions of the far north. But his adventures there served only to whet his appetite for more. Richardson and Back were equally eager to try conclusions once more with the Ice-King in his own domain ; and almost before they had given themselves time to recover their physical strength these three intrepid men volunteered for another expedition to the shores of the Polar Sea. For their second venture they were much better equipped, and therefore they did not encounter nearly so much hardship ; but the same daring spirit was there, and many occasions arose when heroism and resource were called for. Three boats were specially built at Woolwich for this expedition ; and a fourth, the *Walnut Shell*, lightly constructed and covered with india-rubber canvas, was provided for the purpose of crossing rivers, and for easy transportation.

The preliminaries of the expedition were without special interest, and the mouth of the Mackenzie River was safely reached. The great explorer was at this time mourning the death of his first wife, who had died the day after the expedition left England ; and he thus alludes to a pathetic incident in connection with that sad event : " The men had pitched our tent on the beach of Garry Island, and I caused the silk union flag to be hoisted which my deeply-lamented wife had made and presented to me as a parting gift, under the express injunction that it was not to be unfurled before the expedition reached the sea. I will not attempt to describe my emotions as it expanded to the breeze ; however natural, and, for the moment, irresistible, I felt that it was my duty to suppress them, and that I had no right by an indulgence of my own sorrows to cloud the animated countenances of my companions. Joining, therefore, with the best grace I could command, in the general excitement, I endeavoured to return, with corresponding cheerfulness, their warm congratulations on having thus planted the British flag on this remote island of the Polar Sea."

Franklin met his sad bereavement in a brave and uncomplaining spirit, and although its effect upon him was only too painfully evident, he insisted upon continuing his expedition. The whole enterprise was carried through successfully, and he returned to England after an absence of two years and a half, with a vast amount of splendid work to his credit.

But the very fact of his success caused him to be regarded with a curious lack of interest by his fellow countrymen on his return. If he had had a tale to tell of terrible danger, of cruel privation and of hair-breadth escapes from death amid the ice he would doubtless have been the object of a great deal of hero worship. But his story of humdrum and successful work roused no enthusiasm whatever amongst the general public. That it was appreciated by those best qualified to judge, however, is evident from the fact that the University of Oxford conferred upon him the degree of D.C.L. and the king knighted him.

These honours, no doubt, he duly appreciated, but more than all else he would have esteemed the command of yet another Arctic expedition ; for his heart was still set upon the discovery of the north-west passage. Ultimately he was offered such a command, and eagerly accepted it ; but the years that intervened were filled with other and very varied interests.   Into these it is not necessary in these pages to enter—except to record his marriage with Miss Griffin, who had been an intimate friend of his first wife, and whose devotion to her distinguished husband is a matter of history.

After their marriage Sir John and Lady Franklin visited Europe ; and it is recorded that one royal lady at a foreign court was greatly surprised at the appearance of the great explorer when he was presented to her. She had heard, and remembered, the harrowing story of how he had been nearly starved to death in the ice, and had lived for days together on " nasty lichen and strips of hide or old shoes " ; and doubtless she expected to see a thin, cadaverous-looking man, still bearing traces of those early days when he proved by painfully intimate experience that there is " nothing like leather." But the real man was altogether different from the lady's expectation, and she could hardly credit the evidence of her own eyes or ears when a portly, comfortable looking gentleman weighing fifteen stone was introduced to her as Captain Sir John Franklin !

In 1836 Franklin was appointed Governor

THE " TERROR " NIPPED IN THE ICE.

of Tasmania, a position which he held for eight years; and very shortly after his recall in 1844 he heard with delight of a proposal to despatch another expedition to the Arctic regions. The veteran explorer was wildly excited at the news; and as soon as he had satisfied himself that the proposal was actually under consideration he petitioned for the command of the enterprise.

The late Admiral Sherard Osborn, Franklin's biographer, tells us that the great explorer had declared that he considered the command of the proposed expedition to be his birthright, as the senior Arctic explorer in England.

"Directly it was known," says Osborn, "that he would go if asked, the Admiralty were, of course, only too glad to avail themselves of the experience of such a man; but Lord Haddington, with that kindness which ever distinguished him, suggested that Franklin might well rest at home on his laurels. 'I might find a good excuse for not letting you go, Sir John,' said the peer, 'in the record which informs me that you are sixty years of age.' 'No, no, my lord,' was Franklin's rejoinder, 'I am only fifty-nine.' Before such earnestness all scruples ceased. The offer was officially made and accepted. To Sir John Franklin was confided the Arctic expedition consisting of H.M.S. *Erebus*, on which he hoisted his pennant, and H.M.S. *Terror*, commanded by

Captain Crozier, who had recently accompanied Sir James Ross on his wonderful voyage to the Antarctic seas."

The two vessels, specially strengthened, suitably equipped, and provisioned for three years, left Greenhithe on May 19th, and towards the end of July reached a point near Disco in Greenland, where a transport which had accompanied them thus far on their journey, took on board the last letters of officers and crews for home. On July 26th they were seen by a whaler, the master of which reported that they were then moored to an iceberg, waiting for a favourable opportunity to enter the ice of Baffin's Bay. From that day onward not one of that gallant band was ever seen alive, except by wandering tribes of Esquimaux ; and not until 1854 was anything certain gleaned concerning their fate. Even then only the barest facts were obtained ; and it was five years later, in 1859, that his sorrowing countrymen learned, through the memorable discoveries of Sir F. L. McClintock, of the tragedy which had ended the life of Sir John Franklin and his devoted followers.

The story of that tragedy, unfolded through McClintock's brave and loving endeavours, is told in one of the succeeding chapters of this volume.

CHAPTER VIII.

A HERO'S VAIN ᴅ RCH.

ONE of the most heroic ᴜ ᴧᴄtic explorers was Dr. Elisha Kent Kane, a surgeon of the United States Navy; and the story of his expeditions to the Arctic circle in search of Sir John Franklin is full of dramatic interest. Twice, in obedience to his country's call, this intrepid man ventured out to seek for the great English sailor whose fate the whole civilized world yearned to know. In spite of a poor physique, he dared the dangers and the terrors, known and unknown, of a prolonged stay in the terrible, ice-bound polar seas, in order that he might try and discover, if possible, some trace of Sir John and his party.

In all twenty-one expeditions were sent to search for Franklin; of these, three were American; and of these three, two were conducted by Dr. Kane. They are known in the history of Arctic exploration as the Grinnell Expeditions; and from the point of view of popular interest, the second of them is the more notable.

It was on May 30th, 1853, that Dr. Kane set out from the port of New York on his second voyage. He sailed as commander of the *Advance* with a crew of seventeen officers and men, which he afterwards supplemented by the addition of two Greenlanders. His plan was to pass up Baffin's Bay to its most northern attainable point, as far as boats or sledges could reach, to examine the coast-line for traces of Franklin.

Dr. Kane's account of this expedition, contained in an official report which he prepared for the Government of his country, is marked by all the modesty that usually characterizes the brave man ; but those who can read between the lines will be able to see how much of dogged endurance and unflinching heroism is concealed in the plain statement of what was in reality a dangerous undertaking, full of peril and hazard. The following extracts from the report will sufficiently show the character of the work accomplished by this heroic explorer and his nineteen comrades.

From New York the *Advance* proceeded to Melville Bay, and Dr. Kane says : " On reaching that place I found the shore-ice so decayed that I did not deem it advisable to attempt the usual passage along the fast floes of the land, but stood directly to the northward and westward, until I met the Middle Pack." Thence the explorer made for Cape York; but he soon found his progress northward blocked by drifting pack-ice. This he determined to penetrate, though to do so involved considerable danger. First, however, he selected an inlet for a provision depôt in case of future emergency; and buried there a supply of beef, pork and bread. At the same place he deposited the *Francis's* lifeboat from the ship, covering it carefully with wet sand, and overlaying the frozen mass with stones and moss. He and his party discovered long afterwards that the Esquimaux had hunted around this islet; but so skilfully had the *cache* been hidden that even these keen observers had failed to detect it.

The next business was to erect a flagstaff and beacon, near which, by preconcerted arrangement, official dispatches and private letters of farewell were buried; and then the explorer turned his vessel northward, and began his grim fight with the ice. But great masses of it bore down upon the ship, which was being gradually forced towards the south; and so serious did the situation become that at last Dr. Kane was compelled to seek shelter in a land-locked bay, which he appropriately named Refuge Inlet. "We were detained in this helpless situation three valuable days," he says, "the pack outside hardly admitting the passage of a boat. But at last, fearing lest the rapidly-advancing cold might prevent our penetrating farther,

we warped out into the drift, and fastened
to a grounded berg."

It was, however, obviously impossible to
remain in this position for any length of time ;
indeed it was only adopted in order that
advantage might be taken of the first opportunity that offered of getting away from the
ice. Dr. Kane had observed that a small
interspace occurred at certain stages of the
tide between the main pack and the coast ;
and he determined to avail himself of this,
and, if possible, press through it. It was a
proceeding fraught with extreme danger ;
for if he failed in the attempt h's vessel would
be crushed to matchwood between the ice
and the shore. But such was his confidence
in the strength of the *Advance*, and in the
courage and fidelity of his comrades, that he
resolved to take the risk.

The task was such as none but the bravest of
men would have dared to undertake. Whenever the receding tides left them in deficient
soundings the ship was thrown on her
beam ends ; and on two of such occasions
the brig caught fire owing to the impossibility
of securing the stoves in positions of safety.
They got through at last, but the venture had
cost them the loss of part of the starboard
bulwarks, a quarter-boat, the jib-boom, their
best bower anchor, and about six hundred
fathoms of cable.

Winter was now rapidly approaching, and

it was evident that the party must soon be frozen in. The prospect was so hopeless that Dr. Kane's officers addressed to him a written request that he would return to a more southern harbour. But this retrograde movement would have meant the loss of all he had struggled so hard up to this point to gain ; and the fearless explorer simply says of it : " I could not accede to their views. I determined, therefore, to start on foot with a party of observation, to seek a spot which might be eligible as a starting point for our future travel, and, if such a one were found, to enter at once upon the autumn duties of search."

Having thus decided Dr. Kane gave the command of the brig to his first officer, Mr. Ohlsen, and set out with a detachment of his crew, carrying a whaleboat and sledge. The ice soon checked the passage of the boat, which was consequently abandoned ; and the party proceeded with the sledge along a ledge of ice extending for miles beside the edge of the shore. Travel along this ledge of course necessitated following all the indentations of the coast, so that very frequently although many miles were traversed, little real progress was made. Many obstacles and difficulties were encountered, and on one occasion, when crossing a glacier, the whole party was nearly lost. Finally the way became so difficult that even the sledge had to be abandoned, and the journey was continued on foot. The object of the expedition was, however, achieved at last, when Dr. Kane reached a projecting cape, eleven hundred feet high, from which he gained a magnificent prospect of a vast frozen sea to the north and west. What he saw confirmed him in his intention of wintering in the actual position of the brig ; and on his return he proceeded at once to organize parties for the purpose of establishing provision depôts, to facilitate further researches in the spring.

Some idea of the labour involved even in the preliminary work of Arctic exploration may be gathered from the fact that in the selection of sites for three of these provision depôts, and in the transport of stores, the parties engaged in the work passed over more than eight hundred miles of ice.

By the time this work was finished, winter had set in, and further operations had to be postponed owing to the darkness—the unbroken night which, with the awful solitude, makes a sojourn in Polar Seas such a terrible strain on mental as well as physical endurance. The brig had now been frozen in for more than two months—in a position specially chosen for the facilities it offered for scientific observation as well as for procuring water, and for necessary daily exercise.

As the winter was to be passed in a region farther north than had been occupied by any previous expedition, the domestic arrangements for the well-being of the company were studied with special care ; and the need for this becomes apparent when Dr. Kane states that during that terrible winter the sun was for one hundred and twenty days below the horizon ; and owing to a range of hills towards the southern meridian the maximum darkness was not relieved by apparent twilight even at noonday. The cold was so intense that chloroform froze, " and," says the explorer, " we witnessed chloric ether congealed for the first time by a natural temperature."

Before the darkness had thoroughly set in, Dr. Kane tried to ascertain the altitude of the cliffs to the south-west—not an easy matter under such extremely wintry conditions. " Fireside astronomers," he wrote, " can hardly realize the difficulties in the way of observations at such low temperatures. The breath, and even the warmth of the face and body, cloud the sextant arc and glasses with a fine hoar frost."

The return of an exploring party, sent out by D·· Kane for preliminary observations, is thus described in the narrative :

" We were at work cheerfully, sewing away at the skins of some mocassins by the blaze of our lamps, when, toward midnight, we heard the noise of steps above, and the next minute Sontag, Ohlsen and Petersen came down into the cabin. Their manner startled me even more than their unexpected appearance on board. They were swollen and haggard, and hardly able to speak.

" Their story was a fearful one. They had left their companions in the ice, risking their own lives to bring us the news; Brooks, Baker, Wilson and Pierre were all lying frozen and disabled. Where ? They could not tell ; somewhere in among the hummocks to the north and east ; it was drifting heavily round them when they parted. Irish Tom had stayed by to feed and care for the others, but the chances were sorely against them. It was in vain to question them further. They had evidently travelled a great distance, for they were sinking with fatigue and hunger, and could hardly be rallied enough to tell us the direction in which they had come.

" My first impulse was to move on the instant with an unencumbered party ; a rescue to be effective, or even hopeful, could not be too prompt. What pressed most on my mind was, where the sufferers were to be looked for among the drifts. Ohlsen seemed to have his faculties rather more at command than his associates, and I thought that he might assist us as a guide ; but he was sinking with exhaustion, and if he went with us we must carry him.

There was not a moment to be lost. Hurried preparations were made ; the newcomers warmed and fed, while a sledge was

loaded with a buffalo cover, a small tent and
a supply of pemmican. It was decided that,
for the sake of finding the perishing men as
quickly as possible, Ohlsen must accompany
the rescue party, so he was well wrapped
up and put on the sledge, and they started—a
little relief expedition of nine men, including
Dr. Kane. The task before them was no light
one, with the thermometer standing at minus
46 degrees, or 78 degrees below freezing point.
They kept steadily on for sixteen hours, guided
by well-known landmarks and icebergs ; but
at last Ohlsen had to admit that he had
lost his bearings and could guide them no
longer.

"Pushing ahead of the party," says Dr.
Kane, "and clambering over some rugged
ice-piles, I came to a long, level floe, which
I thought might probably have attracted the
eyes of weary men in circumstances like our
own. It was a light conjecture, but it was
enough to turn the scale, for ther˘ was no
other to balance it. I gave orders to abandon
the sledge, and disperse in search of foot-
marks. We raised our tent, placed our
pemmican in *cache*, except a small allowance
for each man to carry on his person, and
poor Ohlsen, now just able to keep his legs,
was liberated from his bag. The thermometer by this time had fallen to minus
49.3 degrees, and the wind was setting in
sharp from the north west. It was out

of the question to halt ; it required brisk exercise to keep us from freezing."

In obedience to their leader's directions, the men proceeded in skirmishing order, but continuously and almost unconsciously kept closing up in a single group as though afraid some disaster was about to overtake them. Dr. Kane himself fainted twice, and several of the others were seized with fainting fits. But after a while they found something that filled them with new hope. One of the party discovered the track of a broad sledge runner, and, carefully following this, they came at length upon " a small American flag, fluttering from a hummock, and lower down a little masonic banner, hanging from a tent-pole hardly above the drift. It was the camp of our disabled comrades ; we reached it after an unbroken march of twenty-one hours. The little tent was nearly covered. As I crawled in, and, coming upon the darkness, heard before me the burst of welcome gladness that came from the four poor fellows stretched upon their backs, and then for the first time the cheer outside, my weakness and my gratitude together almost overcame me. They had expected me, they were sure I would come."

The leader of the rescue party was now confronted with a fresh difficulty. The tiny tent would only accommodate e ght men ; and rescued and rescuers numbered together

fifteen. They were therefore compelled to
take a brief sleep by watches, half the party
walking about outside while the others rested.
When all were sufficiently recovered for the
homeward journey to be attempted, the sick
men were sewn up in reindeer skins and
placed on buffalo robes spread on the sledge,
and then the party set out. Every article
that could by any means be regarded as
superfluous was left behind, but even then
the dead weight that these weary men had
to drag over the hummocky ice was eleven
hundred pounds. Thus burdened they progressed by vigorous pulls and lifts, at the
rate of nearly a mile an hour.

And then one of the most deadly of all the
dangers to be encountered by men exposed
for a long period to extreme cold overtook
them. "Almost without premonition," says
Dr. Kane, " we all became aware of an alarming failure of our energies. I was, of course,
familiar with the benumbed and almost
lethargic sensation of extreme cold, but I had
treated the *sleepy comfort* of freezing as something like the embellishment of romance. I
had evidence now to the contrary. Bonsall
and Morton, two of our stoutest men, came to
me, begging permission to sleep : ' They were
cold ; the wind did not enter them now ;
a little sleep was all they wanted.' Presently
Hans was found nearly stiff under a drift ;
and Thomas, bolt upright, had his eyes

closed and could hardly articulate. At last John Blake threw himself in the snow and refused to rise. They did not complain of feeling cold, but it was in vain that I wrestled, boxed, ran, argued, jeered or reprimanded, an immediate halt could not be avoided.

" With considerable difficulty the few men who were able to exert themselves pitched the tent, and the sick and stupefied men were placed inside. Dr. Kane then went on ahead with one man to the half-way tent and *cache* which they had left behind them on the previous day, hoping to be able to thaw some ice and pemmican in readiness for the others as soon as they should arrive. " I cannot tell," he says, " how long it took us to make the nine miles, for we were in a strange kind of stupor and had little apprehension of time. It was probably about four hours. We kept ourselves awake by imposing on each other a continuous articulation of words ; they must have been incoherent enough. I recall these horrors as among the most wretched I have ever gone through ; we were neither of us in our right senses, and retained a very confused recollection of what preceded our arrival at the tent. We both of us, however, remember a bear who walked leisurely before us, and tore up as he went a jumper that Mr. McGarry had improvidently thrown off the the day before. He tore it into shreds and rolled it into a ball, but never offered to interfere with our progress. I remember this, and with it a confused sentiment that our tent and buffalo robes might probably share the same fate."

When they reached the tent, Kane and his companion were in a state border ng on delirium. They had only just sufficient strength and consciousness to roll themselves in their reindeer sleeping bags, and for the next three hours were oblivious of everything. Then, having somewhat recovered, they roused themselves, melted some ice, and by the time the rest of the party arrived, had some soup ready for them. Having partaken of this, they resumed their journey ; but they were still so weak and exhausted that their leader, having first tried the experiment on himself with considerable benefit, permitted his men to take three-minute naps in the snow, which greatly refreshed them. He also served out small doses of brandy when their strength failed them. Thus, with many halts, they made slow progress, and finally reached the brig in safety.

The sick men were immediately taken in charge by Dr. Hayes, but in spite of all his efforts two of them died. Two others suffered amputation of parts of the foot, and Ohlsen suffered for some time from blindness. The severity of the strain the brave rescue party imposed upon themselves in their efforts on behalf of their comrades may be gathered from the fact that of the seventy-two hours they were out, their halts totalled only eight hours. Four days after the rescue Kane wrote : " I am again at my record of failures, sound, but aching at every joint. The rescued men are not out of danger, but their gratitude is very touching. Pray God that they may live ! "

The terrible winter drew slowly to its end, the fearful monotony of the four months' continuous darkness broken by such amusements as the men could contrive for themselves —a fancy ball ; a newspaper which they called *The Ice Blink* ; and a fox chase round the deck. At last on January 21st came the first faint traces of returning daylight ; but it was three months later before the party could resume active work. Meanwhile they had lost all but six of the magnificent kennel of nine Newfoundland and thirty-five Esquimaux dogs which Dr. Kane had originally possessed, the others having succumbed to a malady which raged amongst them during the winter. Their number was, however, augmented by some new purchases from the Esquimaux, who visited the ship at the beginning of April.

On April 25th Dr. Kane resumed his journey northward, and he remarks on the extreme beauty of the splendid glacier to which he gave the name Humboldt. The explorer's progress was greatly impeded by the snow, which had accumulated in such enormous drifts that the travellers were compelled to unload their sledges and carry the cargo on their backs, beating a path for the dogs to follow in. By slow degrees the party pushed on ; but so great was the effort that Dr. Kane, already enfeebled by the rigours of the winter through which he had passed, was compelled at last to give up.

"I was seized with a sudden pain," says this heroic explorer, "and fainted. Mv limbs became rigid, and certain obscure symptoms of our winter enemy, the scurvy, disclosed the: ves. I was strapped upon the sledge ai   : march continued as usual ; but my pow.) diminished so rapidly that I could not resist the otherwise comfortable temperature of five degrees below zero. My left foot becoming frozen caused a vexatious delay, and the same night it became evident that the immovability of my limbs was due to dropsical effusion. On the 5th, becoming delirious, and fainting every time that I was taken from the tent to the sledge, I succumbed entirely. My comrades would kindly persuade me that, even had I continued sound, we could not have proceeded on our journey. The snows were very heavy, and increasing as we went ; some of the drifts perfectly impassable, and the level floes often four feet deep in yielding snow.

"The scurvy had already broken out among

the men, with symptoms like my own, and Morton, our strongest man, was beginning to give way. It is the reverse of comfort to me that they shared my weakness. All that I should remember with pleasurable feeling is that to my brave companions, themselves scarcely able to travel, I owe my preservation. They carried me back by forced marches. I was taken into the brig on the 14th, where for a week I lay fluctuating between life and death."

Thanks in great measure, doubtless, to the fact that summer was approaching, Dr. Kane was able, with the devoted attention of his comrades, to shake off the serious illness that had gripped him ; but it left him so weak that he was obliged to give up all further sledge excursions for the season and leave others to carry on the work.

The short summer was over all too soon, and little had been accomplished. But, what was worse even than this, the sun had not had sufficient power to melt the icy bonds which still held the *Advance* in a grip as of iron ; and the men were therefore faced with the prospect of another dismal winter in their polar prison. The men were all devoted to their leader ; but they were more or less broken in health, and their store of provision and of fuel was inadequate, so that it is not to be wondered at if they viewed the future with misgiving and dread. Some of them openly declared that they would rather abandon the vessel than face another winter with her.

But their intrepid leader, weaker than most of them, and with more reason therefore to dread the coming months of black night and bitter cold in those desolate solitudes, declared it to be his unalterable purpose to remain. He explained to his assembled comrades that to have abandoned the brig earlier would have been cowardly, and that to do so now was to incur grave risk, since it was only remotely possible to reach the nearest point of civilization before winter was upon them. He left every man free, however, to do as he wished, assuring them that if any chose to leave the ship, and found themselves afterwards compelled to come back, he would give them a brother's welcome on their return. Nine of the seventeen members of the crew chose to go, and they were provided with every appliance for their safety and comfort that the limited resources of the brig could supply. Those who remained seemed inclined to regret that they had not thrown in their lot with their comrades who had gone ; but their indomitable leader gave them little leisure in which to bemoan their lot, and they soon forgot their gloomy fears in busy pre paration for the long, cold night of winter that awaited them. The following is Kane's own account of the position of himself and his comrades at the beginning of that second

winter, and of the plans made for withstand-
ing its gloom and its rigour :

"Our preparations," he says, "were
modified largely by controlling circumstances.
The physical energies of the party had sensibly
declined. Our resources were diminished.
We had but fifty gallons of oil saved from our
summer's seal hunt. We were scant of fuel ;
and our food, which now consisted only of the
ordinary marine stores, was by no means
suited to repel scurvy. Our molasses were
reduced to forty gallons, and our dried fruits
seemed to have lost their efficiency.

"A single apartment was bulk-headed off
amid ships as a dormitory and abiding-room
for our entire party, and a moss envelope,
cut with difficulty from the frozen cliffs,
made to enclose it like a wall. A similar
casing was placed over our decks, and a small
tunnelled entry—the *tossut* of the Esquimaux
—contrived to enter from below. We
adopted as nearly as we could the habits of the
natives, burning lamps for heat, dressing in
fox skin clothing, and relying for our daily
supplies on the success of organized hunting
parties.

"The upper tribes of these Esquimaux
had their nearest winter settlement at a spot
distant, by dog journey, about seventy-five
miles. We entered into regular communication with these rude and simple-minded
people, combining our efforts with theirs for

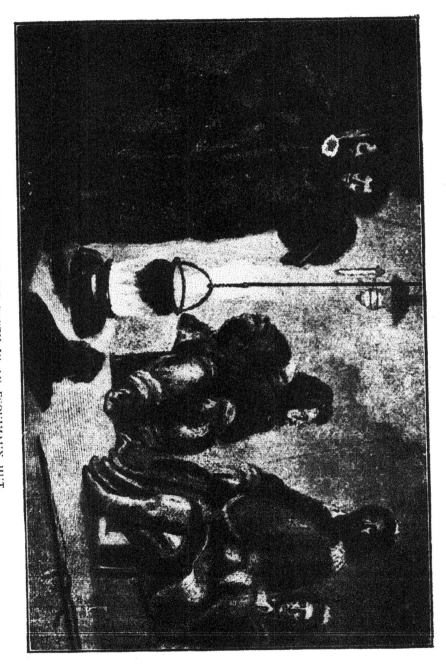

DR. KANE AND HIS PARTY IN AN ESQUIMAUX HUT.

mutual suppor , and interchanging numerous friendly offices. Bear meat, seal, walrus, fox and ptarmigan were our supplies. They were eaten raw, with a rigorous attention to their impartial distribution. With the dark months, however, these supplies became very scanty. The exertions of our best hunters were unavailing, and my personal attempts to reach the Esquimaux failed less on account of the cold (minus fifty-two degrees) than the ruggedness of the ice, the extreme darkness and the renewal of tetanic diseases amongst our dogs. Our poor neighbours, however, fared worse than ourselves ; famine, attended by frightful forms of disease, reduced them to the lowest stages of misery and emaciation.

" Our own party was gradually disabled, Mr. Brooks and Mr. Wilson, both of whom had lost toes by amputation, manifesting symptoms of a grave character. William Morton was severely frozen ; and we were deprived of the valuable services of the surgeon by a frost bite which rendered it necessary for him to submit to amputation. Scurvy, with varying phases, gradually pervaded our company, until Mr. Bonsall and myself only remained able to attend upon the sick and carry on the daily work of the ship, if that name could still appropriately designate the burrow which we inhabited.

" Even after this state of things had begun to improve, the demoralizing effects of continued debility and seemingly hopeless privation were unfavourably apparent amongst some of the party. I pass from this topic with the single remark that our ultimate escape would have been hazarded, but for the often painfully enforced routine which the more experienced among us felt the necessity of adhering to rigorously under all circumstances."

It is probable that Dr. Kane was not greatly surprised when on December 12th the party which had abandoned the ship came back, having failed in their attempt to find safety in the south. They had suffered bitterly from cold and hunger during their wanderings, and doubtless they were rejoiced to get back, and to receive the promised welcome, which was heartily given.

"The thermometer," says D₁ Kane, "was at minus fifty degrees; they were covered with rime and snow, and were fainting with hunger. It was necessary to use caution in taking them below; for after an exposure of such fearful intensity and duration as they had gone through the warmth of the cabin would have prostrated them completely. They had journeyed three hundred and fifty miles; and their last run from the bay near Etah, some seventy miles in a right line, was through the hummocks at this appalling temperature. One by one they all came in and were housed. Poor fellows: as they threw open their

Esquimaux garments by the stove, how they relished the scanty luxuries which we had to offer them. The coffee, and the meat-biscuit soup, and the molasses, and the wheat-bread, even the salt pork which our scurvy forbade the rest of us to touch—how they relished it all! For more than two months they had lived on frozen seal and walrus-meat."

The heroic explorer's welcome to his returning comrades was indeed brotherly and generous. But for him and his brave determination to stay by his ship at all hazards his whole party must inevitably have perished miserably; and it was due to his strong, resolute courage that they were preserved.

Slowly and wearily the interminable hours of that dreary winter of darkness wore away. " February closes," says the heroic explorer. " Thank God for the lapse of its twenty-eight days! Should the thirty-one of the coming March not drag us further downward we may hope for a successful close to this dreary drama. By April 10th we should have seals ; and when they come, if we remain to welcome them we can call ourselves saved. But a fair review of our prospects tells me that I must look the lion in the face. The scurvy is steadily gaining on us. I do my best to sustain the more desperate cases, but as fast as I partially build up one, another is stricken down. Of the six workers of our party, as I counted them a month ago, two are unable to do outdoor work, and the remaining four divide the duty of the ship among them. Hans musters his remaining

two, Bonsall and myself, have all the daily offices of household and hospital. We chop five large sacks of ice, cut six fathoms of eight-inch hawser into junks of a foot each, serve out the meat when we have it, hack at the molasses, and hew out with crowbar and axe the pork and dried apples; attend to the cleansing of our dormitory, and, in a word, cook, *scullionise*, and wait upon the sick. Added to this, for five nights running I have kept watch from 8 p.m. to 4 a.m., catching such naps as I could in the day without changing my clothes, but carefully waking every hour to note thermometers."

In the following month the sufferings of all were aggravated by scurvy, which attacked every man of the party. Usually not more than three of them were well enough to care for the rest, who had to remain in their bunks absolutely unable to stir. Mercifully the leader himself was never quite incapacitated; and to this fact without doubt the whole party owed their lives.

It now became apparent that the abandonment of the ship was an absolute necessity; her upper spars, bulwarks, deck-sheathing, stanchions, bulkheads, hatches, extra strengthening-timbers, in fact everything tha could be taken without destroyii ? her seaworthiness, had a ready been consumec for fuel; and only sufficient food remained for a few weeks. To have attemp'ed to remain a third winter in that dreary region of perpetual ice, while it could have in no way promoted the search for Sir John Franklin, would without doubt have proved fatal to many of the party.

The plans for retreat from their 'cy prison were made with the greatest cai Three boa s—two of them whale boats tw nty-four fee in l gth, and the third a light cedar dinghy c, thirteen fee —were mounted upon runners cut from the cross-beams of the vessel and bolted, to prevent the disaster of breakage. These runners were eighteen feet in length and shod with h p iron. No nails were used in their construction; they were lashed tog ther so as to form a pliable sledge, and upon it the boats were cradled so as to be removed at pleasure. A fourth sledge, wit team of dogs, was reserved for the tra: port of the sick, four of whom were still to move, and for carrying the stock of sions.

A bandoned Esquimaux hut, about thirty e miles from the brig, was fitted up as well as means permitted, as a store, and as a wayside shelter for the accommodation of those of the party who were already broken down, or who might yield to the first trials of the journey. The cooking utensils were extremely primitive ; they consisted of simple soup-boilers, enclosed by a cylinder to protect them from the wind, and they were made from an old stove-pipe. A metal trough to receive fat, with the aid of moss and cotton canvas, enabled the travellers to keep up an active fire.

The provisions, packed in waterproof bags, consisted, with the exception of tea, coffee and small stores for the sick, exclusively of melted fat and powdered biscuit ; and the clothing and bedding was limited to a fixed allowance for each man.

Dr. Kane himself undertook the transport of the sick, and the reserve of provisions, by means of the dog sledge ; and some idea of the labour involved may be gained from the fact that this task alone involved journeyings amounting in the aggregate to eleven hundred miles.

It was on May 17th that the sledge-boats finally left the vessel, dragged over the ice by officers and men ; and so weak and ill were these brave but much tried explorers that during the first eight days their total progress amounted to only fifteen miles. They managed later to proceed at a quicker pace, but their best record never exceeded three-and-a-half miles a day over ice ; and even this was only accomplished at the cost of from twelve to fifteen miles of actual travel.

So commenced what was destined to prove a fifty-six days' journey over ice and water ; and the dangers and hardships involved might well have daunted the stoutest heart amongst them. For they were weakened by famine and disease ; and though they had to contend against neither storms nor drift ice, their boats were so unseaworthy that constant baling was necessary in order to keep them afloat.

As the days passed their weakness increased alarmingly ; their feet became so swollen that they were obliged to cut open their canvas boots ; they were unable to sleep ; and the rowing and baling became hourly more difficult. But these brave, though much tried, men never lost heart, and the supreme courage of their leader was an inspiration to them all. He was kind and considerate to everyone, and especially tender towards the sick ; but he was commander always ; and one point that he insisted upon throughout was that there must be no infringement of the daily routine of work and rest. "We had perpetual daylight," he says; "but it was my rule, rarely broken even by extreme necessity, not to enter upon the labours of a day until we were fully refreshed from those of the day before. We halted regularly at bedtime and for meals." And he adds,

" Prayers were never intermitted. I believe firmly that to these well-sustained observances we are largely indebted for our final escape."

As they moved onward the bulk of their stores decreased, and finally it was found possible to consolidate the party into two boats, the third boat being broken up for fuel, which was badly needed. The leader of the intrepid little band explains that their lengthened practice of alternating boat and sledge management had given them something of assurance in this mode of travel ; and he adds with quite unconscious pathos, " besides, we were familiarized with privation ; it was a time of renewed suffering."

The acuteness of the privation increased as the party moved onward ; and—obviously without in the least intending to do so—Dr. Kane throws a lurid light upon it in the account he gives of his men's capture of a seal, at a time when they were reduced to the verge of starvation. Some of the men caught sight of the animal floating on a small patch of ice, and apparently asleep. " Trembling with anxiety," says the explorer, " we prepared to crawl down upon him. Petersen, with a large English rifle, was stationed in the bow of the boat, and stockings were drawn over the oars as mufflers. As we neared the animal, our excitement became so intense that the men could hardly keep stroke. He was not asleep, for he reared his head when we were almost within rifle shot ; and to this day I can remember the hard, careworn, almost despairing expression of the men's thin faces as they saw him move. Their lives depended on his capture. I depressed my hand nervously, as a signal for Petersen to fire McGarry hung upon his oar, and the boat, slowly but noiselessly surging ahead, seemed to me within certain range. Looking at Petersen, I saw that the poor fellow was paralysed by his anxiety, trying vainly to obtain a rest for his gun against the cut-water of the boat. The seal rose on his fore-flipper, gazed at us for a moment with frightened curiosity, and coiled himself for a plunge. At that instant, simultaneously with the crack of our rifle, he relaxed his long length on the ice, and, at the very brink of the water, his head fell helpless to one side.

"I would have ordered another shot, but no discipline could have controlled the men. With a wild yell, each vociferating according to his own impulse, they urged their boats upon the floe. A crowd of hands seized the seal, and bore him up to safer ice. The men seemed half crazy. I had not realized how much we were reduced by absolute famine. They ran over the floe, crying and laughing, and brandishing their knives. It was not five minutes before every man was mouthing long stripes of raw blubber. Not an ounce of that seal was lost."

Shortly after this incident the north coast of Greenland was reached. On the 6th of August, eighty-three days after leaving the *Advance*, Upernavik was reached, and the toil and danger of the expedition were practically at an end. The object for which it had been organized was not achieved, the fate of the gallant Sir John Franklin still remained a mystery locked in the icy grasp of the Arctic seas ; but it had given the world one more proof that its heroes are ready to dare any dangers for the sake of others.

Although Dr. Kane survived the actual peril of his brave endeavour to trace his great predecessor in the work of Arctic exploration, it is nevertheless sadly true that it cost him his life. He never recovered from the terrible strain and privation of his two winters in the far north ; and two years after his return he died, in the thirty-seventh year of his age, leaving a name worthy of a place upon the honoured roll of those who have sacrificed their lives to the service of science and for the good of their fellow men.

CHAPTER IX.

A TRAGEDY CONFIRMED.

FOR eight years the search for Sir John Franklin, which has now become a matter of history, was continued with unabated vigour by Government and by private enterprise ; but at the end of that time the public authority came to the conclusion that further search was useless ; and in 1857 Lady Franklin was informed that nothing more could be done. The final intimation was conveyed by Sir Charles Wood, who stated " that the members of Her Majesty's Government, having come, with great regret, to the conclusion that there is no prospect of saving life, would not be justified, for any objects which in their opinion could be obtained by an expedition to the Arctic seas, in exposing the lives of officers and men to the risk inseparable from such an enterprise."

But though the Government had given up hope Lady Franklin had by no means done so. She at once began to make preparations for sending out a searching expedition entirely at her own cost. Friends, inspired as much by her pathetic devotion as by their own wish in the matter, came forward with offers of financial assistance, and a sufficient sum for the purpose in view was speedily forthcoming.

The command of the expedition was offered by Lady Franklin to Captain F. L. McClintock, who had already served in three previous search expeditions, and he readily accepted the offer. He applied at once to the Admiralty for leave to undertake the service. Permission was granted, and shortly afterwards Lady Franklin telegraphed to him that he was free to go, and that she had purchased the screw yacht *Fox*, which she placed, with the necessary funds, at his disposal. As soon as it was known that the expedition was actually being organized many distinguished officers eagerly offered their services—amongst them being Lieutenant W. R. Hobson, Captain Allen Young—who not only gave his personal help, but also subscribed five hundred pounds towards the cost of the expedition—and Dr. David Walker, a scientist of great skill and a clever surgeon. "Many worthy old shipmates," says McClintock, "my companions in previous Arctic voyages, most readily volunteered their services, and were as gratefully accepted; for it was my anxious wish to gather around me well-tried men, who were aware of the duties expected of them, and accustomed to

THE MEMORIAL TO SIR JOHN FRANKLIN IN
WESTMINSTER ABBEY.

naval discipline. Hence, out of the twenty-five souls composing our small company, seventeen had previously served in the Arctic seas " A valuable addition to the party was Carl Petersen, so well known in connection with Dr. Kane's expedition, who joined the vessel as interpreter.

The *Fox* was generously provisioned for twenty-eight months ; and towards her stores the Admiralty furnished 6,682 pounds of the indispensable pemmican. It may be of interest here to explain that although there are various methods of preparing this special form of food for the use of explorers, its ingredients never vary. It consists of lean meat, dried and cut into shreds, which is then pounded up, mixed with melted beef fat, and pressed into cases. The Indians of North America—the inventors of pemmican —press the food into prepared gut and skins, so that in their case it resembles nothing so much as a rather solid sausage of comfortable proportions.

At the beginning of July, 1857, the *Fox* commenced her voyage ; and two months later she was in the midst of the Arctic ice, and her crew were contemplating with no little dread the prospect of wintering in the pack, far enough from any point where they could hope to find traces of the ill fated expedition of Sir John Franklin. The dread soon became a reality ; and for the long period of two hundred and forty-two days the *Fox* was held fast in the ice. Captain McClintock made valiant efforts to free his ship, but in vain. She drifted helplessly day after day amongst the giant floes which were packed and piled around her, with no hope of escape, and menaced always with destruction by the huge masses of ice which threatened to close in and crush her.

It is nothing short of marvellous that men can keep their sanity, to say nothing of their courage and hopefulness, under such circumstances. Much of course depends upon the attitude of their commander ; and a significant sentence from McClintock's diary shows how he, at any rate, succeeded in maintaining courage in his men by keeping his fears to himself. " As yet," he says, " the crew have but little suspicion how blighted our prospects are." There is a whole world of heroism in that single sentence. The journal of this truly brave man is full of interest, and supplies a vivid picture of the dangers and privations of an Arctic exploring party ; and in it, moreover, he reveals his own supreme courage, under most depressing conditions, with an unconsciousness that gives his story a peculiar charm.

On August 20th, for instance, he wrote : " No favourable ice drift ; this detention has become most painful. There is no relative motion in the floes of ice, except a gradual closing together, the small spaces and streaks of water being still further diminished. The temperature has fallen and is still below the freezing point. I feel most keenly the difficulty of my position. We cannot afford to lose many more days.

" The men enjoy a game of rounders on the ice each evening. Petersen and Christian are constantly on the look out for seals. They practise an Esquimaux mode of attracting them ; they scrape the ice, thus making a noise like that produced by a seal in making a hole with its flippers, and then place one end of a pole in the water, and put their mouths close to the other end, making noises in imitation of the snorts and grunts of their intended victims. Whether the device is successful or not I do not know, but it looks laughable enough.

" Christian came back a few days ago, like a true seal hunter, carrying his kayak on his head, and dragging a seal behind him. Only two years ago Petersen returned across this bay with Dr. Kane's retreating party. He shot a seal which they devoured raw, and which, under Providence, saved their lives.* Petersen is a good ice-pilot, knows all these coasts as well as, or better than, any man living, and, from long experience and habits of observation, is almost unerring in his prognostications of the weather. Besides his

* This incident is fully related on page 160.

great value to us as an interpreter, few men are better adapted for Arctic work,—an ardent sportsman, an agreeable companion, never at a loss for occupation or amusement, and always contented and sanguine. Happily we have many such dispositions in the *Fox.*

" The whole distance across Melville Bay is 170 miles; of this we have performed about 120, forty of which we have drifted in the last fourteen days.

" Yesterday we set to work as usual to warp the ship along, and moved her ten feet. An insignificant hummock then blocked up the narrow passage. As we could not push it before us, a two-pound blasting charge was exploded, and the surface ice was shattered; but such an immense quantity of broken ice came up from beneath, that the difficulty was greatly increased instead of being removed. This is one of the many instances in which our small vessel labours under very great disadvantages in ice-navigation; we have neither sufficient manual power, steam power, nor impetus to force the floes asunder. I am convinced that a steamer of moderate size and power, with a crew of forty or fifty men, would have got through a hundred miles of such ice in less time than we have been beset."

During the whole of their eight months' imprisonment in the ice they never ceased their struggle to get free. When September

was a week old McClintock confessed that
" to continue hoping for release in time to
reach Bellot's Strait would be absurd; yet,
to employ the men we continued our preparation of tents, sledges and gear for travelling."
Now and then the ice would become more
slack than usual, and a "lane" of water
would appear. On one such occasion a
stretch of only 170 yards of ice separated them
from a lane of this kind. Could they have
reached it they would probably have been
able to extricate themselves completely.
They toiled their hardest, and by the use of
steam and blasting powder they actually
advanced a hundred yards towards the
" lane." Then an adverse wind sprang up
which drove the floes tightly together again,
and all their toil was rendered useless.

Another danger that threatened them came
from the tremendous icebergs that surrounded the ship. One of these, which Allen
Young measured, was 250 feet high, and
aground in 498 feet of water, giving a total
from top to bottom of 750 feet; and the
floe ice drifting past it was crushing up against
its sides to a height of fifty feet. A collision
with one of these enormous bergs would
probably have involved the total destruction
of the ship, and for some days this was a
danger to which they were exposed every
hour. McClintock fully realized the possibility of such a catastrophe; for he says,

" since we first became beset, and consequently the sudden destruction of the ship a contingency which we should be prepared for, provisions have been kept at hand on deck, boats and sledges in readiness for instant use. In such a dire extremity we should, of course, endeavour to reach the nearest inhabited land."

At last, all hope of escaping from the ice was abandoned. "We are doomed," said the commander, "to pass a long winter of absolute inutility, if not of idleness, in comparative peril and privation; nevertheless the men seem very happy, thoughtless, of course, as true sailors always are."

Various devices were adopted for maintaining the happiness of these thoughtless sailors, and one of the most popular was a school, organized by Dr. Walker, who found his pupils very zealous to master the mysteries of the three R's. Indeed their thirst for knowledge became so great that these elementary subjects failed to satisfy them after a time, and they demanded lectures on the trade winds, the atmosphere, the uses of the thermometer, barometer, and so on. McClintock tells with obvious delight how the men took a holiday from school on Guy Fawkes' Day, and organized a procession which marched round the ship with drum, gongs and discord, and then proceeded to burn the effigy of Guy Fawkes. "Their black-

MC'CLINTOCK'S EXPEDITION IN SEARCH OF SIR JOHN FRANKLIN.

ened faces, extravagant costumes, flaring torches, and savage yells frightened away all the dogs ; nor was it until after the fireworks were let off and the traitor consumed, that they crept back again. It was school night, but the men were up for fun, so they gave the doctor a holiday." Christmas was of course a joyous festival, celebrated with feasting, in which the orthodox plum pudding—one of Lady Franklin's many thoughtful gifts,—was a prominent feature ; and the New Year was heralded by the ship's " band," consisting of two flutes and an accordion, which, on this occasion, was augmented by what McClintock terms other "music" from frying pans, gridirons, kettles, pots and pans, in the hands of the crew, who were determined to have as much fun as possible under the circumstances.

So the tedious winter slowly passed, and after months of unbroken darkness the men were greatly cheered by the first gleams of return ng daylight—"not that we were suffering, either mentally or bodily," says their dauntless leader, " but the change is most agreeable, and we can take much longer walks than were possible during the dark period." In their joy at the return of daylight the whole company were perhaps rather more venturesome than they ought to have been ; and on one occas on the commander himself had an unpleasant experience wh ch he thus describes : " A few days ago the ice suddenly cracked within ten yards of the ship, and gave her such a smart shock that everyone rushed on deck with astonishing alacrity. One of these sudden disruptions occurred between me and the ship when I was returning from the iceberg ; the sun was just setting as I found myself cut off. Had I been upon the other side I would have loitered to have enjoyed a refreshing gaze upon this dark streak of water ; but after a smart run of about a mile along its edge, and finding no place to cross, visions of a patrol on the floe for the long night of fifteen hours began to obtrude themselves ! At length I reached a place where the jagged edges of the floes met, so crossed and got safely on board. Nothing was seen during this walk of nearly twenty-five miles except one seal."

It was not until the spring was well advanced, on April 24th, after they had drifted helplessly amongst the ice floes for 1,385 miles, that the gallant little *Fox* was at last in free water. Even then the danger was not entirely past, for the floating ice often dashed against the ship and choked the screw, thus bringing the engines to a dead stop; but compared with the risks of the past months this was but a minor trouble ; and two days later McClintock thus wrote in his journal: "At sea! How am I to describe the events of the last two days ? It has pleased God to accord to us a deliverance in which His

merciful protection contrasts—how strongly—
with our own utter helplessness ; as if the
successive mercies vouchsafed to us during
our long, long winter and mysterious ice-
drift had been concentrated and repeated in a
single act. Thus forcibly does His great
goodness come home to the mind. . . .
We have been brought safely through, and
are all inexpressibly grateful, I hope and
believe."

The summer succeeding that memorable
winter was a busy one for McClintock. He
carefully searched Eclipse Sound, Pond's Bay,
Peel Strait, Regent's Inlet and Bellot's Strait,
but found no trace of the missing expedition.
Still undaunted by disappointment, however,
as summer waned he made arrangements to
pass another winter in the Arctic. This
time, however, he was able to choose his
location, and he fixed upon Port Kennedy, a
harbour of Bellot's Strait, as his headquarters ;
and from this base he and Allen Young, having
made every possible provision for emergencies,
set out in different directions on February
17th, with sledges and searching parties ;
and it was not long before they came upon
traces which enabled them ultimately to find
out the sad fate that had befallen two whole
ships' companies amid the terrors and desolation of the lonely frozen north. The pathetic
details of McClintock's discovery can best be
told in his own graphic words :

"On the 1st of March," he writes, "we halted to encamp at about the position of the magnetic pole, for no cairn remains to mark the spot. I had almost concluded that my journey would prove to be a work of labour in vain, because hitherto no traces of Esquimaux had been met with, and in consequence of the reduced state of our provisions, and the wretched condition of the poor dogs—six out of the fifteen being quite useless—I could only advance one more march.

"But we had done nothing more than look *ahead*. When we halted and turned round, great indeed was my surprise and joy to see four men walking after us. Petersen and I immediately buckled on our revolvers, and advanced to meet them. The natives halted, made fast their dogs, laid down their spears, and received us without any evidence of surprise.

"We gave them to understand that we were anxious to barter with them, and very cautiously approached the real object of our visit. A naval button upon one of their dresses afforded the opportunity. It came, they said, from some white people who were starved upon an island where there are salmon (that is, in a river), and that the iron of which their knives were made came from the same place. One of these men said he had been to the island to obtain wood and iron, but none of them had seen the white men. Another

H. M. S. ships *Erebus and Terror*
{ Wintered in the Ice in

28 of May 1847 { Lat. 70° 5' N Long. 98° 23' W

Having wintered in 1846-7 at Beechey Island
in Lat 74° 43' 28" N Long 91° 39' 15" W after having
ascended Wellington Channel to Lat 77°. and returned
by the West side of Cornwallis Island

Sir John Franklin commanding the Expedition

All well

WHOEVER finds this paper is requested to forward it to the Secretary of the Admiralty, London, *with a note of the time and place at which it was found*; or, if more convenient, to deliver it for that purpose to the British Consul at the nearest Port.

QUICONQUE trouvera ce papier est prié d'y marquer le tems et lieu ou il l'aura trouvé, et de le faire parvenir au plutot au Secretaire de l'Amirauté Britannique à Londres.

CUALQUIERA que hallare este Papel, se le suplica de enviarlo al Secretario del Almirantazgo, en Londrés, con una nota del tiempo y del lugar en donde se halló

EEN ieder die dit Papier mogt vinden, wordt hiermede verzogt om hetzelve, ten spoedigste, te willen zenden aan den Heer Minister van de Marine der Nederlanden in 's Gravenhage, of wel aan den Secretaris der Britsche Admiraliteit, te London, en daar by te voegen eene Nota, inhoudende de tyd en de plaats alwaar dit Papier is gevonden geworden

FINDEREN af dette Papiir ombedes, naar Leilighed gives, at sende samme til Admiralitets Secretairen i London, eller normeste Embedsmand i Danmark, Norge, eller Sverrig. Tiden og Stædit hvor dette er fundet önskes venskabeligt paategnet

WER diesen Zettel findet, wird hier durch ersucht denselben an den Secretair des Admiralitets in London einzusenden, mit gefälliger angabe an welchen ort und zu welcher zeit er gefunden worden ist

Party consisting of 2 Officers and 6 Men
left the Ships on Monday 24th May 1847

SIR JOHN FRANKLIN'S LAST RECORD.

man had been to ' Ei-wil-lik ' (Repulse Bay , and counted on his fingers seven individuals of Rae's party, whom he remembered having seen. . . .

"Despite the gale which howled outside, we spent a comfortable night in our roomy hut.

"Next morning the entire village population arrived, amounting to about forty-five souls, from aged people to infants in arms, and bartering commenced very briskly. First of all we purchased all the relics of the lost expedition, consisting of six silver spoons and forks, a silver medal, the property of Mr. A. McDonald, assistant surgeon, part of a gold chain, several buttons, and knives made of the wood and iron of the wreck ; also bows and arrows constructed of materials obtained from the same source. Having secured these, we purchased a few frozen salmon, some seals, blubber and venison, but could not prevail upon them to part with more than one of their fine dogs. One of their sledges was made of two stout pieces of wood which might have been a boat's keel.

"All the old people recollected the visit of the *Victory*. An old man told me his name was ' Ooblooria.' I recollected that Sir James Ross had employed a man of that name as a guide, and reminded him of it ; he was, in fact, the same individual, and he

inquired after Sir James by his Esquimaux
name of 'Agglugga.' I inquired after the
man who was furnished with a wooden leg
by the carpenter of the *Victory*. No direct
answer was given, but his daughter was
pointed out to me. Petersen explained to
me that they do not like alluding in any
way to the dead ; and that as my question
was not answered, it was certain the man
was no longer amongst the living.'

After an absence of twenty-five days, during
which he had travelled 420 miles, McClintock
returned to the *Fox* and reported to the crew
his partial success. He pointed out, however,
that one of the ships was still unaccounted for,
and declared his intention of resuming the
search. This he did as soon as possible ;
and on June 24th he had the satisfaction of
being able to make the following record in his
journal : " I have now passed on foot through
the only feasible North West Passage ; but
this is as nothing to the interest attached to
the Franklin records picked up by Hobson,
and now safe in my possession. We now
know the fate of the *Erebus* and *Terror*.
The sole object of our voyage has at length
been completed, and we anxiously await the
time when escape from these bleak regions
will become practicable."

But many weeks of painful journeying,
close search and patient inquiry had to elapse
before McClintock could thus write of his task

as accomplished. At Cape Victoria on April 20th he found two families in their snow huts upon the ice. From them he learned that "two ships had been seen by the natives of King William's Island. One of them had been seen to sink in deep water, and nothing was obtained from her, a circumstance at which they expressed much regret ; but the other was forced on shore by the ice, where they suppose she still remains but is much broken.

"The natives told us it was in the fall of the year—that is, August or September—when the ships were destroyed ; that all the white people went away to the 'large river,' taking a boat or boats with them, and that in the following winter their bones were found there."

To avoid snow blindness the party commenced night-marching on May 7th. Crossing over from Matty Island towards the shore of King William's Island, they continued their march southward until midnight, when they had the good fortune to arrive at an inhabited snow village. The natives had probably never seen living white people before, but they were quite prepared to be friendly. At a little distance the party halted and pitched their tent, the better to secure small articles from being stolen while they bartered with the people.

McClintock purchased from these people six pieces of silver plate bearing the crests or

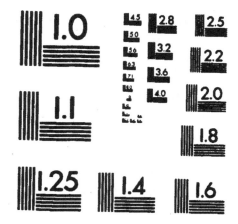

MICROCOPY RESOLUTION TEST CHART
NATIONAL BUREAU OF STANDARDS
STANDARD REFERENCE MATERIAL 1010a
(ANSI and ISO TEST CHART No. 2)

initials of Franklin, Crozier, Fairholme and McDonald ; they also sold their bows and arrows of English wood, uniform and other buttons, and offered them a heavy sledge made of two short stout pieces of curved wood, which no mere boat could have furnished them with ; but this of course could not be taken away. The silver spoons and forks were readily sold for four needles each.

The extreme friendliness of the people made the bartering an easy matter ; and the narrative continues : " Having obtained all the relics they possessed, I purchased some seal's flesh, blubber, frozen ven son, dried and frozen salmon, and sold some of my puppies. They told me it was five days' journey to the wreck—one day up the inlet still in sight, and four days overland. This would bring them to the western coast of King William's Island ; they added that but little now remained accessible of the wreck, their countrymen having carried almost everything away. In answer to an inquiry they said she was without masts ; the question gave rise to some laughter amongst them, and they spoke to each other about *fire*, from which Petersen thought they had burnt the masts through close to the deck, in order to get them down.

" There had been many books, they said, but all had long ago been destroyed by the weather ; the ship was forced on shore in

RELICS OF SIR JOHN FRANKLIN.

the fall of the year by the ice. She had not been visited during the past winter, and an old woman and a boy were shown to us who were the last to visit the wreck ; they said they had been at it during the preceding winter.

" Petersen questioned the woman closely, and she seemed anxious to give all the information in her power. She said many of the white men dropped by the way as they went to the Great River ; that some were buried and some were not ; they did not themselves witness this, but discovered their bodies during the winter following."

Evidence of the fate of Franklin was thus accumulating, but McClintock, desirous of obtaining absolute proof, made further search ; and as a result he found a small cairn, twelve miles from Cape Herschel, in which he discovered a note, stating that Franklin had died on June 11th, 1847. Thus the melancholy fate of one of the best and bravest of England's sons was proved beyond all question, and McClintock's sad task was accomplished.

He received the well deserved honour of knighthood for his services ; but perhaps the reward that touched him most was the presentation handsome gold chronometer, subscribed for by the officers and crew of the *Fox*.

Many of Franklin's relics of pathetic interest were found subsequently by other travellers and explorers, and the most precious of these, as well as those discovered by McClintock, are preserved in Greenwich Hospital, where they bear to-day their mute testimony to the heroic endurance of some of the bravest men of Britain's race.

CHAPTER X.

FOR many years after McClintock had placed the fate of Franklin beyond all doubt, the search for traces and relics of the great explorer was continued ; and amongst the many notable and successful voyages undertaken for this object was that organized by Charles Francis Hall, an American of great experience in Arctic exploration. He subsequently undertook an expedition to the North Pole which was suddenly and tragically terminated by his death from over exertion caused by a long sledge journey. His party, deprived of their leader, made preparations to return as quickly as possible ; but their vessel, the *Polaris*, was caught in the deadly grip of an impassable icepack, and for two months drifted helplessly.

After eight weeks of incessant grinding and crushing amongst the ice, a furious storm added to the peril of the situation ; and the crew of the ship, convinced that complete destruction awaited them if they remained on board, made preparations to encamp on a huge ice floe to which they had attached their vessel, and on which they had some time previously built an ice house. The reality of the danger which forced them to this desperate expedient can best be appreciated from the following account of the effect of the storm upon the ship :

"The *Polar* ⸱⸱⸱; driven along at a very rapid rate. ⸱. · ⸱er faces looked over the rail and pee ⸱ ⸱· the darkness and the gloom, wonde. ⸱_ what would happen next. Two icebergs were passed in close proximity, and one could scarcely help shuddering as he thought of the consequences of running into one of those gigantic ice-mountains.

" In the morning the vessel ran amongst some icebergs, which brought up the floe to which she was attached. At the same time the pack closed up, jamm'ng her heavily ; and it was then the ship received her severest nip. It is hard to describe the effect of that pressure. She shook and trembled. She was raised up bodily and thrown over on her port side. Her timbers cracked with a loud report, especially about the stern. The sides seemed to be breaking in. The cleat to which one of the after hawsers was attached snapped off, and the hawser was secured to the mast. One of the firemen, hurrⱽing on deck, reported that a piece of ice had been driven through the side."

Escape from destruction seemed to be impossible. The pressure and the noise increased together. The violence of the storm, the darkness of the night and the grinding of the ice added to the horror of the situation.

Feeling that it was extremely doubtful whether the ship would stand the strain, Captain Bud ngton ordered provisions and stores to be thrown upon the ice. Then followed a busy scene. Each one was deeply impressed with the danger of the situation, and exerted himself to the utmost. Boxes, barrels, cases, were thrown over the side with extraordinary rapidity. Men performed gigantic feats of strength, tossing with apparent ease, in the exc tement of the moment, boxes which at other times they would not have attempted to lift. Forward, coal and the more substantial provisions and bags of clothing were thrown overboa, d ; abaft, the lighter boxes of canned meat and tobacco, with all the musk-ox skins and fresh seal meat, were transported to the floe. The cabin was entirely emptied ; beds and bedding, clothes, and even ornaments, were carried out ; and boxes containing all the notebooks and observations were also secured.

There were many Esquimaux, men and women, with the expedition ; and in this crisis the women worked as hard as the men. All their labour, however, could not delay even for a moment the catastrophe that was now imminent. The increasing pressure of the surrounding ice caused the great floe itself to crack in several places; and the supreme calamity occurred when two of these cracks ran through the places where the stern anchors had been planted, thus breaking their hold.

The wind, still strong, now drove the vessel from the floe; and the anchors dragging under the strain, she swung round to the forward hawser. The latter slipped and the vessel was carried rapidly away from the ice. The night was black and stormy, and in a few moments the floe and its precious freight could no longer be seen through the drifting snow.

Before the separation it had been noticed by the men on the ship that the floe was much broken on its edge; that the heaps of provisions and stores were separated by rapidly widening cracks; that the men also were on different pieces of ice; that active efforts were being made to launch boats in order to bring the scattered people together. Several men were seen rushing towards the ship as she was leaving, but they failed to reach her; and as she floated away the voice of the steward, John Herron, was heard calling out "Good-bye, *Polaris* !"

The men left on the ship—fourteen in number—were almost in sorrier plight than those on the floe, for their vessel was leaking so badly that it was impossible for her to remain long afloat ; they had scarcely **any** food, no bedding, and no clothing but what they were actually wearing. Fortunately it was not long before they reached land ; and with the help of a number of friendly Esquimaux they built a house on shore, and finally abandoned the *Polaris* when they had taken from her all that could be of use to them.

From the wreckage of the ship they contrived to build two sailing boats, and ultimately, after eight months of great peril and privation, they managed to travel far enough southward to come within the tracks of the whalers, by one of which they were ultimately rescued and brought safely to land.

But this narrative has mainly to do with the unfortunate castaways who were left adrift on the ice floe. Including the Esquimaux contingent they numbered nineteen souls. Their position, though sufficiently appalling, was not altogether hopeless ; for, provided the floe did not break up they would be able to maintain life for considerable time, with the stores that had so hurriedly thrown overboard from *Polaris*. The ship's boats were also with them, and in these the men, stores, provisions and records that had been carried off on broken pieces of the floe at the moment of the great catastrophe were gathered together and brought back to the main floe.

After a tempestuous night the men took to the boats, intending to make for the nearest land, and search for the *Polaris* ; but a stiff breeze sprang up, and the work of navigating their frail craft through the loose ice proved so dangerous that they were obliged to return and haul their boats up on to the floe again. Shortly after this they actually saw the *Polaris* rounding a point some ten miles distant, under steam and sail. They made desperate efforts to attract the attention of those on board but without avail, and the ship dropped out of sight behind a headland.

Owing to continual breaking of the ice the floating home of these poor derelicts was becoming rapidly smaller, and their alarm may be imagined when they found it had shrunk to only a hundred and fifty yards each way.

Their store of food, too, decreased so rapidly that extreme economy soon became a vital necessity ; and had it not been for the occasional capture of a seal the speedy death of the whole party from starvation would have become inevitable. It is pitiful to learn that these poor people refrained from exercise on the score of economy, since they found that much movement added to their hunger.

The winter days and nights of unbroken darkness were passed in the snow huts which they had built ; and the intolerable monotony was only relieved by occasional hunting—a difficult and dangerous occupation in the season of perpetual night. They were fortunate in the possession of instruments which enabled them to keep count of time, and the coming of Christmas was hailed with joy as an excuse for indulging in a little extra food. At breakfast on the day of the festival an additior d ounce of bread made the soup a little thicker than usual. At dinner there was soup again, made of seal's blood, a car. of sausage meat and a can of apples, half a pound of ham and two ounces of bread. The menu does not sound attractive, but Herron says in his journal it was the sweetest meal he ever ate.

The new year opened drearily, with the grim spectre of starvation ever drawing nearer; but in spite of their terrible condition, the little party managed to maintain a cheerful demeanour, and the occasional capture of a seal saved them from despair when hope grew faint and death seemed very near. Day followed day, with no other excitement than the success or failure of the hunters ; and at last, as the winter season neared its end, and the temperature became less severely cold, a new menace had to be faced; for the ice floe which had been their home for so long showed unmistakable signs of breaking up. " The floe was surrounded by insecure icebergs, and during the whole of one night the sounds proceeding from its cracking and working were like those of artillery, preventing sleep. The ice seemed likely at any moment to break into pieces ; and so alarming was the cracking of the floe a night or two later that the people remained up and dressed, and kept themselves and all their necessaries of life ready, in case of a sudden d꞊ꞇster."

By the end of March it became necessary to abandon the floe ; and the entire party of twelve men, two women and five children embarked in the only boat they then possessed— a frail thing intended to carry six or eight men only. So heavily was she overloaded that these all but starving people were compelled to throw overboard one hundred pounds of meat and nearly all their clothing, retaining only their tent, a few skins for protection, and a little meat, with the small remainder of their bread and pemmican.

For days they drifted about amongst the pack ice, landing now and then on a floe which seemed large and substantial enough to offer them safety for a time with an opportunity of making a fire and so securing the advantage of a warm meal ; but they were never really safe on the floes even for an hour ; and hairbreadth escapes were of frequent occurrence. During one terrific storm, while they were encamped on a floe, the ice split across the tent in the early morning, while the men were getting out a few ounces of pemmican. They saved themselves, but came near losing their boat, and actually lost their breakfast. The storm continued some days, and while it lasted seal-hunting was out of the question. There was no blubber to feed the lamp, and therefore there was no water to drink. The prospect was gloomy indeed. Half of the men lay down in the tent to get a little rest ; while the remainder walked around it ; but for those who attempted to rest the body there was no repose for the mind. One after another would spring up from his place and make a wild dash forward, as if to avoid some sudden danger.

While this storm was at its height, one of the party—Meyer—nearly lost his life. The ice broke between the tent and the boat, which were so close that there was not space to pass between them ; and Meyer, with the boat and the kayak, was separated from the rest of the party. A stinging wind was driving the snow with keenest force ; it was bitterly cold ; the ice was cracking and grinding with a very heavy sea.

" Meyer cast the kayak adrift, in the hope that it would reach the other part of the floe, and that Joe or Hans (two of the Esquimaux) might come in it to his assistance ; but it drifted away to leeward. The natives took their paddles and ice-spears and went after it, springing from piece to piece until, by propelling a small piece of ice, they got near enough to Meyer to catch a rope which he threw to them, and with which he dragged them toward him.

" In the meantime, those who remained behind watched Meyer and the natives with the extremest anxiety, and could just make out through the darkness that they had reached him. Nothing more could be done during the night ; it was necessary to wait for daylight, which happily came at 3 a.m. On remembering that it was impossible for the three to manage the boat by themselves, others determined to join them. In order to do so they were obliged to make the same perilous journey. This they accomplished in safety, and brought the boat back, after a long struggle, to the original floe. The kayak also was saved.

" Meyer and Jamka (another of the Esquimaux) had fallen into the water during the night, but luckily there were two or three dry shirts for them. All of the men were more or less wet ; Meyer, having been very wet all night, came near being frozen to death. He lost his breath for some time, but Joe and Hans labouring diligently, succeeded in rousing him from his lethargy, and finally he was restored to full consciousness by violent exercise. Shortly afterwards he found that his toes were frozen.

The sufferings of these forlorn castaways were mitigated for a few hours, when the storm abated ; but at best their condition was desperate ; and it was not long before the sea rose again menacingly and in a little while their steadily dwindling ice floe was in such a condition that " there was not a dry place to stand on, nor a piece of fresh water ice to eat, the sea having swept over everything, and filled the depressions where fresh water ice was sometimes found." And all the time the grim spectie of starvation haunted them. There were days together when no animal life of any kind approached them, and sometimes when a seal appeared the skill of the Esquimaux, who were of course expert hunters, was not equal to catching it, and the starving people were thus tormented with the prospect of food which after all eluded them.

But gradually their floe was drifting southward ; and the knowledge that they were slowly but steadily drawing nearer to the track of the whalers, and thus increasing their hope of rescue, was the one thing that sustained them. And at last there came a day when a steamer was sighted. Frantic with joy, the people on the floe made strenuous efforts to attract the steamer's attention, but without avail. The vessel held on her course, night descended, and all hope of rescue was for the time at an end.

Two days later another steamer was seen, and the party, collecting all their rifles and pistols, fired them together to attract attention. Three rounds were fired, and then the steamer answered with three shots and headed for the floe. But she failed to find the castaways, and finally steamed off in another direction.

Even then, however, these brave-hearted people did not lose heart. They knew now that they must be well in the track of the whalers and they felt sure they must be rescued soon. And their confidence was not misplaced. A day or two after their second disappointment, another steamer was seen close to the floe. The guns were fired, the colours were set on the boat's mast, and loud shouts were uttered. Hans shoved off in his kayak, of his own accord, to intercept her if possible. The morning was foggy, but the steamer's head soon turned towards them, and in a few moments she was alongside of the floe.

The three cheers given by the shipwrecked people were returned by a hundred men on deck and aloft. The vessel proved to be the *Tigress*, a sealer, from Newfoundland. Her small seal boats were very soon in the water ; but the shipwrecked party did not wait for them. They threw everything out of their own boat, launched her, and in a few moments were on board the *Tigress* where they became objects of extreme curiosity, as well as of the most devoted attention. When the time during which they had been on the ice was mentioned, they were regarded with astonishment, and warmly congratulated upon their miraculous escape.

That theirs was indeed a marvellous deliverance is manifest ; and the story of such protracted suffering of so extreme a kind so bravely borne, is one of the most pathetic of the many stories of heroism and endurance associated with the peril which the voyager has to face in his journeyings 'mid snow and ice in the far north.

CHAPTER XI.

AN ADVENTURE WITH AN ICEBERG.

IT has already been made clear that one of the gravest dangers that ships in the Arctic circle have to meet is that which arises from possible contact with an iceberg. These huge masses of floating ice, often weighing many thousands of tons, are a constant menace to the vessels of explorers. If a ship collides with one, destruction is almost inevitable ; and to be caught between two is simply to be crushed out of existence. The danger of such a catastrophe, and the fear it inspires in the heart of the sailor, is well illustrated in the following thrilling narrative of an incident which actually occurred during a voyage in an emigrant ship, driven out of her course to the far north. The story is related by a member of the crew.

"For ten days we had fine weather and light winds, but a southerly gale sprang up and drove us to the northward, and I then found out what it was to be at sea. After the gale had lasted a week the wind came round from the northward, and bitterly cold it was. We then stood on rather farther to the north than the usual track, I believe.

"It was night, and blowing fresh. The sky was overcast, and there was no moon, so that darkness was on the face of the deep—not total darkness, it must be understood, for that is seldom known at sea. I was in the middle watch—from midnight to four o'clock —and had been on deck about half an hour, when the look-out forward sang out : 'Ship ahead ! Starboard—hard a starboard ! '

"These words made the second mate, who had the watch, jump into the weather rigging.

" ' A ship ! ' he exclaimed. ' An iceberg it is, rather ! All hands wear ship ' : he shouted, in a tone which showed there was not a moment to lose.

"The watch sprang to the braces and bow-lines, while the rest of the crew tumbled up from below, and the captain and other officers rushed out of their cabins. The helm was kept up and the yards swung round, and the ship's head turned towards the direction whence we had come. The captain glanced round and then ordered the courses to be brailed up, and the main topsail to be backed, so as to lay the ship to. I soon discovered the reason for these manœuvres, for before the ship wore round, I perceived close to us a towering mass with a refulgent appearance, which the look-out man had taken for the white sails of a ship, but which proved in reality to be a vast iceberg ; and attached to it, and extending a considerable distance to leeward, was a field, a very extensive floe of ice, against which the ship would have run had it not been discovered in time, and would, in all probability, instantly have gone down, with every one on board.

"In consequence of the extreme darkness it was dangerous to sail either way ; for it was impossible to say what other floes, or smaller cakes of ice, might be in the neighbourhood, and we might probably be on them before they could be seen. We therefore remained hove to. As it was, I could not see the floe till it was pointed out to me by one of the crew.

"When daylight broke the next morning the dangerous position in which the ship was placed was seen. On every side of us appeared large floes of ice, with several icebergs floating, like mountains on a plain, amongst them ; while the only opening through which we could escape was a narrow passage to the north-east, through which we must have come. What made our position the more perilous was that the vast masses of ice were approaching nearer and nearer to each other; so that we had not a moment to lose if we would effect our escape.

"As the light increased we saw at a distance of three miles to the westward, another ship in a far worse predicament than we were, inasmuch as she was completely surrounded with ice, though she still floated in a sort of basin. The winds held to the northward, so that we could stand clear out of the passage, should it remain open long enough. She by this time had discovered her own perilous condition, as we perceived that she had hoisted a signal of distress, and we heard the guns she was firing to call our attention to her; but regard for our own safety compelled us to disregard them until we had ourselves got clear of the ice.

"It was very dreadful to watch the stranger, and to feel that we could render her no assistance. All hands were at the braces, ready to trim the sails should the wind head us; for in that case we should have to beat out of the channel which was every instant growing narrower and narrower. The captain stood at the weather-gangway, conning the ship. When he saw the ice closing in on us he ordered every stitch of canvas the ship would carry to be set on her, in hopes of carrying her out before this should occur. It was a chance whether or not we should be nipped. However, I was not so much occupied with our own danger as not to keep an eye on the stranger, and to feel deep interest in her fate.

"I was in the mizzen top; and as I possessed a spy glass I could see clearly all that occurred. The water on which she floated was nearly smooth, though covered with foam caused by the masses of ice as they approached each other. I looked. She had but a few fathoms of water on either side of her. As yet she floated unharmed ; the peril was great ; but the direction of the ice might change, and she might yet be free. Still, on it came with terrific force, and I fancied that I could hear the edges crushing and grinding together.

"The ice closed on the ill-fated ship. She was probably as totally unprepared to resist its pressure as we were. At first I thought that it lifted her bodily up ; but it was not so—I suspect she was too deep in the water for that. Her sides were crushed in ; her stout timbers were rent into a thousand fragments, her tall masts tottered and fell, though still attached to the hull. For an instant I concluded that the ice must have separated, or, perhaps, the edges broken with the force of the concussion ; for as I gazed the wrecked mass of hull and spars and canvas seemed drawn suddenly downward wit' irresistible force, and a few fragments whic had been hurled by the force of the concussion to a distance, were all that remained of the hapless vessel. Not a soul of her crew could have had time to escape to the ice.

"I looked anxiously ; not a speck could be seen stirring near the spot. Such, thought I, may be the fate of every being on board this ship ere many minutes are over.

"I believe I was the only person on boaɪ who witnessed the catastrophe. Most of tl emigrants were below ; and the few who wɩ on deck were, with the crew, watching o own progress. Still narrower grew the passa_ Some of the parts we had passed through w already closed. The wind, fortunately, h fair ; and though it contributed to drive ɩhɩ ice faster in upon us, it yet favoured our escape. The ship flew through the wa r at a great rate, heeling over to her ports ; but though at times it seemed as if the masts would go over the sides, still the captain held on. A minute's delay might prove our destruction.

"Everyone held his breath as the width of the passage decreased, though we had but a short distance more to make good before we should be free.

"I must confess that all the time I did not myself feel any sense of fear. I thought it was a danger more to be apprehended for others than for myself. At length a shout from the deck reached my ears, and, looking round, I saw that we were on the outside of the floe. We were just in time ; for the instant after the ice met, and the passage through which we had come was completely closed up. The order was now given to keep the helm up and to square away the yards, and, with a flowing sheet, we ran down the edge of the ice for upwards of three miles before we were clear of it.

"Only then did people begin to enquire what had become of the ship we had lately seen. I gave my account, but few expressed any great commiseration for the fate of those who were lost. Our captain had had enough of ice, so he steered a course to get as fast as possible into more southern latitudes."

CHAPTER XII.

A WILD DRIVE ON A DOG SLEIGH.

AN almost indispensable adjunct to the work of the Arctic explorer is the Esquimaux dog—a breed as famous in its way as that of St. Bernard. Its usefulness in the regions of perpetual snow is well known ; and it is not too much to say that without the aid of this sagacious, hardy animal, much of the most valuable work of Arctic explorers could never have been attempted. It is appropriate, therefore, that some account of this four-footed native of the north, with, later, a story of a desperate ride in which several of his kind played an important part, should find a place in these pages.

The dog of the Esquimaux possesses a sturdy and muscular figure, thick, furry hair, and a bushy tail, curled gracefully over the back. Its voice, at least in its native climate, is not a bark, but a long, melancholy howl ; though when it is brought to England, and associates with others of its kindred, it soon follows their example.

There is a remarkable adaptation on the part of this creature to the service of the people whose country is one of boundless deserts of snow, whose winter endures for three-fourths of the year, and whose climate has an intensity of cold which description can scarcely convey. As a race inhabiting the Arctic regions, and being dependent for their subsistence and clothing on the produce of the chase, the Esquimaux look to their dogs for assistance in the pursuit of the seal, the bear and the reindeer. Nor is this all; they yoke them to heavily laden sledges, which, with untiring patience, these animals will often draw fifty or sixty miles a day.

When drawing a sledge the dogs have a simple harness of deer skin or seal skin going round the neck by one bight, and another for each of the forelegs, with a single thong leading over the back, and attached to the sledge as a trace. Though they appear, at first sight, to be huddled together without regard to regularity, considerable attention is, in fact, paid to their arrangement, particularly in the selection of a dog of peculiar spirit and sagacity who is allowed, by a longer trace, to precede the rest as a leader; and to whom, in turning to the right or left, the driver usually addresses himself. This choice is made without regard to age or sex; and the rest of the dogs take precedence according to their training or sagacity, the least effective being put nearest the sledge.

The leader is usually from eighteen to twenty feet from the fore part of the sledge, and the hindmost dog is about half that distance ; so that, when ten or twelve are running together, several are nearly abreast of each other. The driver sits quite low on the fore part of the sledge, with his feet over-hanging the snow on one side, and having in his hand a whip, of which the handle, made of wood, bone, or whalebone, is eighteen inches, and the lash as many feet in length. The part of the thong next the handle is plaited a little way down, to stiffen it and give it a spring, on which much of its use depends ; and that which composes the lash is chewed by the women, to make it flexible in frosty weather.

The men acquire from their youth considerable expertness in the use of this whip, the lash of which is left to trail along the ground, by the side of the sledge ; and with which, at pleasure, they can inflict on any dog a very sharp blow. Though the dogs are kept in training entirely by the fear of the whip—and, indeed, without it would soon have their own way—its immediate effect is always detrimental to the speed of the sledge ; for not only does the individual that is struck draw back and slacken his trace, but generally turns upon his next neighbour ; and this, passing on to the next, occasions a general divergency, accompanied by the usual yelping and showing of the teeth. The dogs then come together again by degrees, and the speed of the sledge is accelerated ; but even at the best of times, by this rude method of draught, the traces of one third of the dogs form an angle of thirty or forty degrees on each side of the direction in which the sledge is advancing.

Another great inconvenience attending the Esquimaux method of harnessing the dogs, besides that of not employing their strength to the best advantage, is the constant entanglement of the traces, by the dogs repeatedly doubling under from side to side, to avoid the whip ; so that after running a few miles the traces always require to be taken off and cleared.

In directing the sledge, the whip plays no very essential part ; the driver for this purpose uses certain words, as the carters do with us, to make the dogs turn to the right or to the left. To these words a good leader never fails to respond, especially if his own name be repeated at the time, looking behind over his shoulder with great earnestness, as if listening to the directions of the driver. On a beaten track, or even where a single footprint or sledge mark is occasionally discernible, there is not the slightest trouble in guiding the dogs ; for even on the darkest night and in the heaviest snowdrift there is little or no danger of their losing their road, the leader keeping his nose near the ground, and directing the rest with wonderful sagacity. When, however, there is no beaten track, the best driver amongst them makes a very circuitous course, as all the Esquimaux roads plainly show ; these generally occupying an extent of six miles, when, with a horse or sledge, the journey would scarcely have amounted to five.

On rough ground, as amongst hummocks of ice, the sledge would frequently be over-turned or altogether stopped if the driver did not repeatedly get off, and, by lifting or drawing it to one side, steer clear of such accidents. At all times, indeed, except on a smooth and well made road, he is constantly thus employed with his feet. which, together with his never-ceasing vociferations, and frequent use of the whip, renders the driving of a sleigh by no means a pleasant or easy task.

When the driver wishes to stop the sledge he calls out " *Wo, woa !* " exactly as our carters do ; but the attention paid to this command depends altogether upon his ability to enforce it. If the weight is small, and the journey homeward, the dogs are not to be thus delayed. The driver is therefore obliged to dig his heels into the snow to obstruct their progress; and, having thus succeeded in stopping them, he stands up with one leg before the foremost cross piece of the sledge, till, by means of laying the whip over each dog's head, he has made them lie down. He then takes care not to quit his position, so that should the dogs set off, he is thrown upon his sledge, instead of being left behind by them.

With "good sleighing," six or seven dogs will draw from eight to ten hundredweight, at the rate of seven or eight miles an hour, for several hours together. With a smaller load, they will run ten miles an hour, and are, in fact, almost unmanageable. To the women who nurse them when ill, and treat them with greater kindness than the men, they are affectionate in the highest degree ; and though from the men they receive little except blows and ill-treatment, they are still faithful and enduring.

In the chase, these dogs know no fear, and in combat they are undaunted. They will fasten eagerly on the most ferocious bear ; discover a seal-hole by the smell at a great distance ; and, even ﹖ yoked to a sledge in which the hunter is ﹒ted, they will chase the reindeer with so much energy as to bring the prey within reach of the unerring bow. In one instance only do they show the influence of fear ; of the wolf they have an instinctive terror, which manifests itself on his approach, in a loud and long-continued howl.

ESQUIMAUX SLEDGE AND DOGS.

These dogs have borne their part in many a stirring adventure 'mid ice and snow ; and a thrilling story in which they figure is related by the Rev. Egerton R. Young, a medical missionary who for years laboured amongst the natives of the Arctic regions. " On one occasion," says Dr. Young, " I received this startling message : ' Come at once and come as quickly as you can, for I have taken an overdose of quinine, and am afraid I will die of hydrophobia.'

" This unique communication was brought to me one wintry day by an Indian hunter, from a distant Indian settlement two hundred miles away.

" The writer of it was an Indian native helper, who had been placed in temporary charge of a mission station until an ordained missionary could be secured to take full charge of the place. This native worker was not destitute of ability or zeal, but he had the misfortune to get hold of a medical volume that gave a rather vivid description of many of the ills to which the human frame is subject. The Indian, who had quite a good knowledge of the English language, read this book with a feeling of horror. He was fascinated by it. It nearly frightened him out of his wits. He fancied he was the possessor of nearly every disease therein described.

" With all the medicines with which I

had furnished him to heal the sicknesses of the people, he liberally dosed himself, until, from their effects upon him, he really became sick. This, of course added to his horror and alarm. He neglected his work, and spent his time in feeling his pulse, looking at his tongue in the glass, and industriously dosing himself with every variety of drug in his possession. The climax was reached when he took an overdose of quinine. The word 'hydrophobia,' to him incomprehensible, seemed at the time a fitting word to represent his fears, as well as his feelings, and hence his remarkable epistle.

" As speedily as possible I prepared three trains of dogs. Our sleds were heavily loaded, the principal parts of the loads being food supplies for this Indian and his household.

" I secured a capital Indian guide, whose duty was to run on his snow-shoes ahead of our dogs in the right direction. There was but little vestige of a road, as frequent blizzard storms swept through those northern wastes and forests, and obliterated any trail that might have been made by passing hunters.

" As is customary and essential in travelling with dogs in that country, we had with us, on our sledges, our kettles, provisions, bedding, guns, and everything absolutely necessary to living out in the open air, independent of the rest of the world. We did not see a house on the whole route, and only met with a few hunters, through whose hunting grounds we passed. Three times, when night overtook us, we made our camp in the woods and there slept with no roof over us.

" Abundance of fur robes and warm blankets made our wintry beds under the stars. We spent the nights as best we could. Sometimes, as there we slept, the clouds arose, and from them a heavy fall of snow silently covered us, like a great warm blanket, and added much to our comfort.

" After various adventures and mishaps, incident to such lands and such methods of travel, we reached the southern end of a lake about thirty miles long. On the northern end of this lake was situated the mission where lived my hypochondriacal Indian, towards whose house we were travelling. As it was about sundown when we come in sight of the lake, and there was abundance of good wood for a winter camp, we decided to spend the night there and go on in the morning. However, ere we had unharnessed our dogs, we heard the shouts of some Indians, and the merry jingling of dog bells.

" It did not take long for my men to notify these strangers of our presence, and very speedily we were joined by them. To our surprise we found that the party consisted of my afflicted friend, and a couple of Indian dog-drivers. They each had a train of very large, fierce-looking Esquimaux dogs. On my expressing my pleasure and satisfaction at seeing him so much better than I expected, judging by his letter, he replied that the medicine book had told him that his disease would run its course in so many days, and so he thought that while it was doing so he would just run up and see me about it.

" My Indian companions, whom I had prepared for the probably imaginary character of his ills, wanted, as I did, to laugh at him ; but we managed to keep our faces straight while he told us of the various diseases that had assailed him since we had seen him six months before.

" I comforted him with the assurance that I had not only food and other supplies in my dog sledges for him, but medicine that would speedily drive out of him all his diseases. This latter piece of information so delighted him that he at once proposed that I should give it to him then and there. However, this was not my plan for curing such a case of what the French call *mal imaginaire,* and so I decided that it would be much more effective and thorough if we waited until we returned to his home. This did not satisfy him, and then I had to tell him that I must insist on delay.

" As a compromise, however, it was decided that after a good supper at the camp fire, now brightly burning, we would continue the journey, instead of camping there for the night.

" The trail most of the way had been very difficult. Our loads were heavy, and our dogs were so tired that they were in no humour for rapid travelling. It seemed almost cruel to push on, but this man with all of his imaginary ills, could think of no delay.

" To judge by his appearance and energetic actions, he was the healthiest man in the crowd. My Indians would have objected to continue the journey if the stalwart invalid had not so eloquently detailed his multitudinous troubles.

" So it was resolved that we should go on, and as the lake was covered with fairly smooth ice the travelling would now be so much easier for the dogs.

" The frozen lakes and rivers always give us our best roads for dog travelling. On the sick man discovering that I had my medicines with me in my own cariole, he made a proposition to exchange dog trains with me for that home run. This was the cause of my exciting adventure and trouble.

" His dogs were large, powerful Esquimaux, full of life and mischief. He had abundance of fish, and so his dogs were in as fine condition as could be.

" For days they had been kept tied up, in preparation for this long journey of two hundred miles on which he had started. The thirty miles run on the ice from his home to this place, where we had met, had really only limbered up such animals for their work.

"Our sleds were all re-packed and some of the heaviest bundles placed on those of the Indians who had met us. My tired dogs were unfastened from my cariole, and in their place was attached the train of four fierce Esquimaux.

"My own faithful, cautious guide, as he carefully tucked the warm fur robes around me in the cariole, handed me a heavy dog-whip, and said that in all probability I would have to use it, if those dogs found out that they were dragging a white man. This whip had a heavy oak handle, less than two feet long, while the heavy well-shotted lash was over fifteen feet in length.

"The sick man, the owner of these dogs, as he straightened them out in the trail on the ice, with their faces towards home, said to me:

"'Now, do not speak a word and there will be no trouble. They will run you to my home in less than three hours. They will keep on the trail we have made in coming on the ice, even if there has been but little snow in which to mark it. They do not like white people, but if you do not speak to them, in their anxiety to get home, they will never suspect.'

"I looked the fierce brutes over, and then

so placed my heavy whip that I could instantly seize it if necessary, and made up my mind that I was in for a wild, exciting ride.

"It was a glorious night. The sun had gone down in unclouded splendour, and now the stars were shining with a beauty and clearness that can only be witnessed when there is no fog, or mist, or damp. The intense cold had cleared away all such obstructions. Before us was the great frozen lake, stretching away far beyond the distant horizon. To my inexperienced eye there was on that icy expanse not the vestige of a road. Yet during the long hours of this intensely cold night, without a single companion, I was going to trust myself to the care of four Esquimaux dogs, to run me thirty miles to a lonely log house on the distant shore. During those long hours I was neither to cough nor speak a single word for fear of trouble, or perhaps a fierce battle with these savage brutes; and if it should take place, who could tell which side would win in the conflict? No wonder my spirits rose, and I felt this was a trip of no ordinary interest.

"With the consolatory words of my guide that after resting the weary dogs for an hour or two they would follow in my trail, and with the hope that they would find me safe at the end, my adventurous journey was suddenly begun by the owner of the dogs vigorously applying his whip on them, which of course, started them off on a furious gallop.

"It was indeed a glorious ride. The well-trained dogs were splendidly matched, and so in perfect unison they dashed along. My cariole was about ten feet long, and eighteen inches wide. Its bottom was made of inch oak boards, and its sides were of parchment. I sat well back in the rear end, and was so well muffled in furs that only my eyes were visible. So narrow was my cariole that a certain amount of balancing was necessary when dashing over occasional snow-drifts, which at times are found even out on the great frozen lakes. But I had become used to this work, and so had no fear of an upset. For about fifteen miles we thus sped on. The dogs would sometimes drop into a swift trot and then again resume their rapid gallop. They were on the home stretch, and so required no further incentive to urge them along.

"It was a unique ride, and exhilarating in the extreme. To add to the splendour of the starry heavens the wondrous Auroras came dancing and flashing and blazing up before me in the northern sky. They formed into great armies and fought out their ghostly battles with no rude sounds to disturb the northern solitudes. Then, when apparently satisfied with this performance, they rolled across the heavens in great ribbons of light,

from which they flung out long flags of purest
white, which seemed as flags of truce from
heaven to earth. Then suddenly, with all
the rapidity of electrical phenomena, they
changed to pink and yellow and then to blood-
red crimson, until the whole heavens seemed
aglow with vivid colours so intense that the
snowy particles on the ice caught the reflection,
and when we dashed through them it seemed
as though they were pools of the blood of thousands slain. Then again there was another
transformation, and now, as from the regions
of departed spirits, there noiselessly flitted
into dim vision the ghostly, shadowy forms
of multitudes clad in purest white or in robes
of pink or yellow. In rhythmic measure they
danced along not far above the horizon, and
then with a sudden bound they flew up into
the heavens above us, only pausing in the
midway course for a second to flash out in
some more glorious colour, or to be transformed
into forms of more ravishing beauty. When
the zenith was reached the grandest transformation of all took place, for here came whole
multitudes of what seemed to have been
those who had been engaged in the carnage
of blood, to the pure, white-robed houris,
innocent spirits of light, untainted by sin or
stain. In myriads they came, and, as though
every one knew its place they rapidly formed
in the very zenith above us, the crowning
glory of the auroral displays, the perfect

corona of beauty, the grandest vision the
eye of man ever gazed upon.

"How it blazed and scintillated and shone
above us!—the perfect crown of splendour,
the one corona of beauty : fit diadem for
Him ' on Whose head are many crowns.'

"Then, as the whole corona blazed out in
equal brightness all over its glittering surface,
the shadow of my dogs was thrown completely
under them. These ghostly shadows seemed
to startle and stimulate their pace, as to the
sole music of their little bells they rapidly
sped along. They seemed also to startle
something else, for out from a rocky island
on our left there dashed a splendid black
fox. He was indeed a beauty, and so vivid
was the Aurora, that I had a very fine view
of him as he rapidly hurried across our trail
and struck out for a well-wooded, rocky island
perhaps half a mile on our right.

"The sight of him very much excited my
dogs. Home and their comrades and kennels
were for the time forgotten, and away from
the home trail they dashed in wild, mad
excitement after that fox. How far they
would run in the pursuit, I could not tell;
but every moment was taking us farther from
the trail, and, if it were once lost, could we
find it again ?

" Thus I had to do a lot of thinking in a very
short time and quickly decide what to do.
We had come about half the distance and

there were at least fifteen miles to run before us, and it was not safe to be madly racing after a fox out on this great lake. So I resolved to break the silence and to turn those dogs into the home stretch, even if I had to fight them then and there. The preparations necessary were not many. Quickly bracing myself on my knees with my robes well around me, I gripped the heavy whip so that I could, if necessary, use the handle of it as a club. Then I sternly shouted to the dogs in Indian to stop, and then turn to the left. The instant they heard my voice they did stop, and that so suddenly that my rapidly moving cariole went sliding on and passed the rear dog of the train as far as his traces would allow. Then they furiously came for me. The leader of the train was the fiercest of the four, and he led in the attack. It was well for me that he did so, as, swinging the others around, they were in such a position that only one of them could reach me at the same time. I am left-handed, and so as he sprang at me I guarded my face with my right hand, well wrapped in the furs, while I belaboured him over the head with the oak whip-handle. Three or four well-administered blows were all he wanted, and with a howl he dropped on the ice, while the next one in the train tried his best to get hold of me. One fortunate clip on the side of his head sent him tumbling over on his leader, and then I had

to face the third one of the train. He proved
the ugliest customer of all, and I never before
imagined a dog's head could take such a
pommelling ere he would give in. Failing
to get hold of me, he tore the robes and parchment side of the cariole. It was well for me
that the traces of the fourth dog, fastened to
the front of the cariole, held him back, so that
he was unable to do more than savagely
growl at me, while he at times fastened his
teeth into every th:ng within reach. His
efforts, however, kept the car:ole twisting in a
most erratic fashion, and so I had to keep
up the fight and at the same time look well
to my balance so as to not be upset.

" With the third dog conquered, I uncoiled
the long lash of the whip, and, shouting
' Marché! ' I vigorously and promiscuously
used it on them. They did not wait for many
applications, but speed ly sprang to their
feet. The leader wheeled around to the left,
and away they flew. At first they seemed
tangled up in the traces, but trained dogs are
wonderfully clever in straightening out from
these mix-ups, and so it was then. On they
sped to the left, until their sharp scent at once
indicated when the home trail was reached,
and then the home journey was once more
resumed. I had no hesitation in speaking now.
As my voice, in unison with the pistol-like
reports of the whip, rang out, they showed no
more desire for battle, but a desperate resolve

to reach home as speedily as possible. But ere the journey ended they played me a shabby trick, and in a measure got their revenge on me.

" At the bottom of the hill on which the house of this native agent was built, he had dug a trench and there fixed a heavy stockade to assist in breaking the wild storms that swept over the lake and drifted the snow around his home. This stockade was fifteen or eighteen feet high. The storms had so piled up the snow on the lake side that it was now level with the top, while over the other side there was only a drift of about five or six feet in depth.

" There was a regular dog trail around by the gate to the house ; but, of course, I knew nothing about this. The dogs knew, however, and were always accustomed to use it. But this night, as though furious and revengeful at the white man who had conquered them, when we arrived within a few yards of the house, they, instead of taking the usual route, dashed up this long, packed snow-drift on the lake side and sprang with me over the high stockade into the drifts beyond. It was a wild, mad leap of over ten feet. Fortunately the snow into which we plunged was deep enough to break the force of the fall ; but, as it was, I felt the effects of it for weeks. Madly the dogs struggled out of the snow-drift ; then up the hill they hurried with me to the house.　Sharp ears had heard our coming, and familiar hands grasped the dogs and led them away, while I was taken by a half frightened woman into the Mission Home among her equally alarmed little ones, who required any amount of explanation why a pale-face had come in that way with their father's dogs.　I was thankful to be under a roof once more, and after a time was able, especially by the presents which I had brought, to make friends of all the household.

"The rest of the party arrived during the night.　The medicines administered to the sick man proved efficacious, and he at this ·date is still alive and vigorous."

CHAPTER XIII.

OVER THE INLAND ICE.

A NAME that will always be held in high honour in the records of Polar exploration is that of Fridtjof Nansen. His first acquaintance with the far north was made in 1882, when as a young zoologist, intent on an investigation of the habits of Arctic animals, he accompanied the *Viking*, a Norwegian sealer, on a voyage to the east coast of Greenland.

The ship became locked in the ice; and as day succeeded day and the vessel slowly and helplessly drifted nearer and nearer to the bleak and rocky shore, Nansen became possessed with a desire to land ar. . explore the unknown waste that lay beyond. The prospect was not an inviting one, and it could have appealed to none save a born explorer ; but the idea took such a strong hold of the young zoologist that at last he sought the captain and asked his permission. But leave was sternly refused. The captain agreed that it might be possible to reach the shore by walking over the close packed ice as Nansen suggested; but he pointed out that the ice might at any time yield and release the ship. The moment that happened he wanted to proceed to the sealing ground; and he would not risk the possibility of having to delay his business in order to await the return gf his passenger from a land-trip. So, with oreat reluctance the idea was given up. But only temporarily. The prospect of exploring that part of the coast of Greenland—whereon, so far as he knew, no European had ever yet set foot—fascinated him; and he determined that one day he would find out the secrets of that undiscovered country.

But he was sensible enough to know that for the present his dream was impossible of fulfilment; and on his return to Norway he very wisely settled down to work, and found congenial occupation as curator of the museum at Bergen. There he remained for four years, and then he decided that if he could achieve his purpose in no other way he would fit out a little expedition at his own expense. Friends persuaded him, however, that his scheme was of national importance, and so he applied to the Government of his country for the financial help he needed. It was not forthcoming; but a Danish gentleman Herr Gamél, hearing of the young enthusiast's difficulty, generously sent him the sum he needed.

With the necessary funds in hand Nansen lost no time in making his preparations. His plan was to travel on ski, the long snow shoes which most Norwegians can use expertly ; for he believed that by this means the ground he intended to explore could be covered with comparative ease. He secured for his companions on the journey three of his fellow countrymen—Otto Sverdrup, Oluf Dietrichson and Kristian Kristiansen—all, like himself, expert in the use of the ski ; and in addition he obtained the services of two Lapps—Ole Ravna and Samuel Balto.

The equipment of the expedition was an important matter, which involved long and serious consideration ; for on this its success or failure would largely depend. But at last all was ready—sledges (which the adventurers decided they would draw themselves), ski, tent, bedding, clothing, food, guns and ammunition, scientific instruments, medicines and various indispensable odds and ends—and the travellers set out on what many of their friends regarded as a mad-brained undertaking.

Nansen travelled by Copenhagen and London to Leith, where he joined the rest of the party, who had preceded him straight to that port with all the baggage. From Leith they went to Iceland, where Nansen had arranged with the captain of a Norwegian sealer, the *Jason,* to take them as far as the east coast of Greenland and either land them on the shore, or as near the shore as the floe ice would permit.

That ice of this kind may prove a formidable obstacle to the voyager who seeks to land on an Arctic shore is made very clear by Nansen's striking description of it. " As to its large features," he says, " it is just their overpowering simplicity of contrast which works so strongly on the observer's mind ; the drifting ice, a huge, white, glistening expanse, stretching as far as the eye can reach and throwing a white reflection far around upon the air and mist; the dark sea, often showing black as ink against the white ; and above all this a sky now gleaming cloudless and pale blue, now dark and threatening with driving scud—or again wrapped in densest fog—now glowing in all the rich poetry of sunrise or sunset colour, or slumbering through the twilight of the summer night. And then, in the dark season of the year, come those wonderful nights of glittering stars and northern lights, playing far and wide above the icy deserts, or when the moon, here most melancholy, wanders on her silent way through scenes of desolation and death. In these regions the heavens count for more than elsewhere ; they give colour and character, while the landscape, simple and unvarying, has no power to draw the eye.

" Never shall I forget the first time I

entered these regions. It was on a dark night, and ice was announced ahead. I ran on deck and gazed ahead, but all was black as pitch and indistinguishable to me. Then suddenly something huge and white loomed out of the darkness and grew in size and whiteness, a marvellous whiteness in contrast to the inky sea, on the dark waves of which it rocked and swayed. This was the first floe gliding by us. Soon more came gleaming far ahead, rustling by us with a strange, rippling sound and disappearing again far behind. As I looked I heard a curious murmur to the north, like that of breakers on a rocky coast, but more rustling and crisper in sound. The sound came from the sea breaking over the floes while they collided and grated one against the other. We drew nearer and nearer, the noise grew louder, the drifting floes more and more frequent, and now and again the vessel struck one ´. another of them. With a loud report the floe reared on end, and was thrust aside by our strong bows. Sometimes the shock was so violent that the whole ship trembled, and we were thrown off our feet upon the deck.

" Then one evening it blew up for a storm, and as we were tired of the sea we resolved to push into the ice and ride out its fury there. So we stood straight ahead ; but before we reached the margin of the ice the storm fell upon us. Sail was still further shortened

till we had but the topsails left, but we still
rushed inwards before the wind. The ship
charged the ice, was thrown from floe to floe,
but on she pushed, taking her own course in
the darkness. The swell grew heavier and
heavier, the floes reared on end and fell upon
each other; all around us was seething and
noise. We bored steadily inwards, into the
darkness. The water seethed and roared
round our bows ; the floes were rolled over,
split in pieces, were forced under or thrust
aside, nothing holding its own against us.

" Then one looms ahead, huge and white,
and threatens to carry away the davits
and rigging on one side. Hastily the boat
which hangs in the davits is swung in on to the
deck, the helm is put down and we glide by
uninjured. Then comes a big sea on our
quarter, breaking as it nears us, and as it
strikes us heavily we hear a crash and the
whistling of splinters about our ears. A
floe has broken the bulwarks on the weather
side. The ship heels over, we hear another
crash, and the bulwarks are broken in several
places on the lee-side, too."

Through this surging sea of huge fragments
of floating ice progress was slow and dangerous, and considerable difficulty was experienced in finding a possible landing place ; but
at last this was accomplished ; the travellers
were lowered into boats over the side of the
Jason, and pulled for the shore. But their

troubles were not yet at an end. More than once their shoreward way was hopelessly blocked with ice, and they were obliged to drag the boats on to some great floe.

For twenty-four hours they worked hard— mostly in pelting rain, which added greatly to their discomfort, and at the end of that t'me they had the mortification of finding themselves about twice as far from the shore as when they had left the *Jason*. But against almost overwhelming obstacles they per- severed. For several days they drifted helplessly at the mercy of the currents, now this way, now that, amongst the ice floes, but never shorewards for long together ; and Nansen found to his dismay that on the whole their direction was towards the south. But at last their persistence was rewarded ; for one morning Nansen woke to find one of the Lapps excitedly shouting at his tent door, " Land very near ! " It was indeed true. During the night the great ice-pack had opened, and the floe which had served the party for a craft had drifted through and was steadily nearing the beach. Without delay the tent was struck and the boats launched ; and before long the men had the joy of finding themselves once again on land.

The first business of the voyagers was to prepare for themselves a feast to celebrate their landing; and after twelve days on an ice floe, subsisting on cold, raw food and snow-water, the prospect of a hot meal was specially alluring. As soon as the feast was finished they took to the boats again and resumed their journey ; for already a great part of the summer was over ; and if the Inland Ice was to be crossed before winter set in Nansen knew he had not an hour to lose.

The next day they came upon a couple of Esquimaux—friendly little men—who willingly escorted them to their settlement. The travellers and the natives were mutually interested, but Nansen and his party found little to admire in the home life of the East Greenlanders. The tents of the people are suffocatingly hot and stuffy, and the stench of the oil lamps which provide light and heat is intolerable.

For ten days the travellers pushed on, sometimes rowing over open water, but more often fighting their way through the ice, and ultimately they reached Umivik, the point at which Nansen had decided to abandon the boats and commence his journey over the Inland Ice to Christianshaab.

Some time was spent in overhauling the sledges and ski, and in securing the boats and provisioning them, in case the party might be forced to turn back and retreat by way of the coast. Then when all was ready a start was made.

The snow being soft and sticky in the day time, it was decided to travel by night ;

and at nine o'clock on the evening of August 15th the men harnessed themselves to their sledges and started off. The way was all uphill, and so steep that it took three men to draw each sledge, so that for some time progress was very slow. The men, too, had for so long been cramped up in the boats, with no chance of using their legs, that they found the unaccustomed exercise very trying; and after a march of only three miles they had to halt for rest and food.

When a few hours later they resumed their march they found their progress greatly impeded by crevasses which, covered with snow, formed traps into which the unwary were continually falling. Rain, too, proved a great hindrance, stopping them sometimes for days together; and Nansen at last felt compelled to reduce the rations since, with these unexpected delays, it was impossible to tell how long their journey to the west coast might take.

At last the way became so bad that Nansen decided to turn back, and try to find another road. This involved further delay for the time bei: but it proved an advantage in the end; foi little to the northward they found the ice l broken and the way not so steep. But still the work of dragging the sledges over the rough ice was exhausting; and the absence of water and the consequent difficulty of assuaging thirst was a severe trial. Every man carried under his coat a tin flask filled with snow, which melted with the warmth of his body ; but the water thus obtained was scanty, and never sufficient to quench the thirst of the travellers.

In spite of all the difficulties of the way the party kept steadily on, still always ascending, until they reached an elevation of six thousand feet. Nansen never feared that his intention of crossing Greenland would fail— his only anxiety was lest he should not reach the west coast in time for the last steamer, which he knew left Christianshaab for Copenhagen about the middle of September. As the days passed anxiety turned to certainty, and the explorer had to face the fact that he could not possibly reach Christianshaab soon enough. Being, however, a man of resource, and very much averse to the alternative of wintering in Greenland, he decided to make for Godthaab, a nearer point on the coast, from which it might still be possible to catch a ship.

The direction of travel was therefore changed ; and in order to expedite progress the sledges were lashed together, a couple of tarpaulins were utilized as sails, and they went sailing over the snow-covered ice in a way that roused the Lapps to great admiration and amazement. As the season advanced the cold increased, and sometimes even when the sun was shining brightly snow was falling as fine as frozen mist ; and when to this a keen wind was added the conditions of travel became supremely uncomfortable. It was no uncommon thing for the travellers to find that their boots, upper and under socks were all frozen together in one solid mass ; and the risk of frost bite was in those days a danger to be reckoned with.

Early in September a furious snow-storm was encountered ; and so thick were the whirling flakes that it was impossible to see more than a yard or two ahead. On the second day of the storm the march was shortened and the tent pitched earlier than usual. It was only with extreme difficulty that the tent was raised at all ; and so fierce was the storm that the snow penetrated through the joints and fastenings of the canvas to such an extent that cooking was entirely out of the question. In order to provide themselves with a little extra warmth, some of the party removed their outer clothing and attempted to don extra under garments ; and the difficulty and misery of such an undertaking in a cold tent, with drifting snow over everything, may be imagined.

All night the storm raged with unabated fury, and in the morning it showed little signs of having spent itself ; but so eager was Nansen to push on towards Godthaab that he resolved to try and proceed. One of the Lapps, Balto, made his way with difficulty out through the drifted snow which almost completely blocked the doorway of the tent, but he quickly came in to say that a march that day was out of the question. Nansen, however, was so anxious to move forward, that he determined to investigate personally ; but when he had seen for himself the whirling tempest of snow he realized that to venture out into it would be simply to court death.

So fierce became the storm that day that the party began to fear for the safety of the tent, and some of them set to work to strengthen it, while others ventured just outside to the sledges to fetch in further stores of provisions. The two Lapps, strangely enough, were the only despondent members of the party, and gloomily prophesied the death of everybody in the tent ; but the others laughed them out of their fears, and on the whole the time passed not unpleasantly.

By the following morning the storm had nearly spent itself, and the travellers having breakfasted and dug their tent out of the snow, in which it was nearly buried, started once more on their way.

It is very difficult for those who have had no actual experience of an Arctic snowstorm to imagine what it is really like. The Russian artist Borissoff, who went through desperate ventures in the land of snow and ice, to bring back what he saw upon canvas, painted a picture entitled " The Snowstorm

Approaches," and to his picture he appended the following note :

" Snowstorms are of a terrible nature in these regions. I often started with my sleigh, drawn by dogs or reindeer, without even being able to distinguish the dogs or the reindeer before me. The safest thing to do was to reach a rock as fast as possible, in order to get shelter. The native, terrified by fright and superstition, wraps his fur coat around him, and lies down on the rock right in the snow. He gets up every fifteen minutes in order to remove the snow from his dogs and sleigh. As long as the snowstorm lasts, three days sometimes, he stays on the same spot, almost frozen and starved to death, but he is of a robust constitution, and as soon as the storm is over, and if the dogs have not perished with cold, he returns home ; when deprived of his dogs he accomplishes the journey on foot ! "

Nansen and his party found progress through the newly fallen snow, which lay soft and deep, difficult and tedious ; and so tiring did it prove that frequent halts for rest and refreshment were necessary. The dietary of the party was necessarily restricted, but thanks to their leader's foresight they managed to contrive considerable variety. Breakfast consisted of chocolate or tea, biscuits, potted liver, and pemmican. This meal was usually served to the party in their sleeping bags by the unfortunate member whose duty it was to prepare it ; and this chilly task usually fell to the lot of either Nansen himself or Balto, who proved to be the best cooks of the party. After breakfast the business of striking camp was accomplished with all speed, and then came a couple of hours of hard sledge-pulling, unless the weather conditions were favourable for sailing. Then came a brief halt, when each man was served with a cake of meat chocolate, and after this another spell of work preceded dinner, which consisted usually of potted liver, pemmican, oatmeal biscuits, and—of all things!—dessert. This was a special compound of Nansen's own invention, and he was very proud of it. It was made of snow, citric acid, oil of lemons, and sugar; and the inventor's companions voted it excellent.

Dinner over, marching was again resumed with as little delay as possible, and two hours later another halt was called, and meat chocolate was again served out.

On the strength of this the party marched again, the next halt being for five o'clock tea, consisting of biscuits, potted liver and pemmican. After tea came more marching, relieved by one more cake of meat chocolate per man, till finally the welcome order was given to halt for the night. Then, the tent being pitched, supper was prepared, this meal usually including tea, soup, or stew, in addition to the inevitable pemmican and biscuits. Thus it will be seen that the travellers fortified themselves with food seven times a day ; and although he was consumed with anxiety to get on, Nansen probably made greater progress in spite of his frequent stoppages than if he had adopted the policy of forced marches and allowed fewer halts for rest and refreshment.

Supper was the only leisurely meal of the day, and even this seldom occupied more than an hour. When it was finished the party made such preparations as were necessary for the next morning, and then, burying themselves in their sleeping bags, were soon sound asleep.

The appliances considered indispensable by the scullery maid of civilization necessarily have no place in the outfit of an Arctic explorer, and Nansen's party could rarely spare water even for washing out their cooker, in which soup, tea and stew were prepared quite impartially. But hard work in a freezing atmosphere soon inures men to mixed flavourings ; and if the tea sometimes tasted of stew, or the soup had a suggestion of tannin, no one minded ! On one occasion Nansen, always trying to devise culinary novelties, experimented with citric acid in the tea ; but everybody forgot the chemical consequence of adding acid to milk. The tea was duly sugared and milked in the usual way ;

but when the citric acid was introduced a heavy curd was at once formed which sank to the bottom of the cup. The men's opinion of the mixture was strong, and they expressed it forcibly. Nansen, however, being above all things a man of courage, drained his cup to the bitter dregs, and pronounced it very good. But the experiment was not repeated.

The dragging of the heavy sledges over the snow proved such exhausting work that after a time Nansen found it necessary to lighten the loads as far as possible ; and amongst other things that he decided he would dispense with was some oil-cloth that had been brought to preserve their sleeping bags from damp. He was about to throw this away when it occurred to him that it ought to burn well ; and as fuel was none too plentiful he resolved to make a fire with it to heat some water. The experiment, however, was not altogether a success . " The fuel burned bravely," says Nansen ; " the flames rose high, and shed a fine glow on the six figures which were grouped around, and sat gazing at the blaze and enjoying the real solid comfort of a visible fire. It was the first time we had had a fire of this sort inside the tent, which wanted something of the kind to make it really cosy. But all the joys of life are fleeting, and none have I known more fleeting than that which comes from burning oil-cloth in a tent which has no outlet in the roof. Our fuel smoked to such an extent that in the course of a few minutes our little habitation was so full that we should scarcely have been able to see one another if we could have kept our eyes open, which we could not do, as the pain caused by the fumes was simply insupportable.

"If there be a mortal who has seen the inside of a barrel in which herrings are being converted into bloaters, he will be able to form some idea of the atmosphere of our tent. Our pleasure at the sight of the fire had long died out ; the eye that managed to open could only see a faint light glimmering far away in the fog."

Nansen had now accomplished half, and that the harder half, of his journey. Hitherto his progress had been a steady ascent, until on September 11th his camp was pitched at a height of 8,250 feet above sea level. At this elevation the cold, as may be imagined, was intense ; but the spirits of the men never flagged ; and now the prospect before them of a gradual descent to the coast heartened them considerably. As they slowly reached lower levels the air became appreciably warmer ; and after six days of travel their hearts were cheered by the twittering of a bird—a snow-bunting—the first indication that they had at last left the desolate region of eternal snowy silence behind them. That bird was the first living thing the men had heard or seen for a month ; and those who have not experienced the absolute sound- lessness of an Arctic solitude can hardly imagine the relief that comes to the traveller in those regions with the first indication of living nature.

After a time, a favourable breeze having sprung up, the tarpaulin sails were once again rigged up on the sledge and the whole party went merrily sailing over the snow. This method of progression was full of excite- ment, and not without its dangers to .en who were not accustomed to steering sledges driven by the wind. On one occasion Nansen was himself tumbled off ignominiously when trying to secure an·ice-axe which had got loose from its fastenings on top of the load. Once, too, it was only his wonderful skill and presence of mind that saved the flying sledge and its human freight from disappearing for ever in a huge crevasse that suddenly yawned in front of him. That happened on a day when, anxious to make every possible use of the breeze that was sending them along, they travelled after sunset by the light of the moon. As they were rushing along Nansen suddenly caught sight of a dark shadow in front ; " but the next moment," he says, " when I was within no more than a few yards I found it to be something very different, and n an instant swung round sharp and brought the vessel up to the wind. It was high time, too, for we were on the very edge of a chasm broad enough to swallow comfortably sledges, steersman and passengers. Another second and we should have disappeared for good and all. We now shouted with all our might to the others, who were coming gaily on behind, and they managed to stop in time." Such an impressive reminder of the risk they ran was not to be ignored ; so the whole party at once halted for the night.

The next morning, to their great joy, the travellers found that they were in front of the great expanse of coast to the south of Godthaab Fiord. They were not yet, however, at their journey's end, although the goal was almost in sight, and a good deal of arduous and dangerous work still awaited them. Many crevasses in the ice proved exceedingly troublesome ; and a storm of hail compelled them to take down their sails and haul the sledges—a task which involved such hard labour that an early halt was deemed advisable. Instead of camping on land that night, as they had hoped to do, they were obliged once more to pitch their tent on the ice.

Next morning the hail storm had changed to a veritable tempest of snow, through which it was only possible to creep slowly, feeling at almost every step of the way for the treacher·ous crevasses that might otherwise engulf them at any moment.

In the midst of a whirl of snow t' at b is
out everything beyond a yard o' two ahead of
the traveller it is impossible to k ep an
exact course; and when, towards afternoon, the
storm abated somewhat, Nansen realised that
he was considerably farther to the northward
than he had intended to go. The course
was therefore alter d, and the party presently
found themselves in a narrow defile between
progress
with the sledges exceedingly difficult. The
storm too came on again with r newed fury,
nd at length a halt was called, a l the Lapps
vere le to pitch the tent and prepare supper.
while the others vent forward to see what
lay ahead.

They had not gon far when Nansen saw
in front a dark patch vhich he imagined to be
clear ice. On a nea approach, however,
it proved to be water—a pool of clear, sweet
water, the first the travellers had seen for
weeks. Down on their knees they went, and
a mon t later they were sucking in great
oughts of it. From that time onward they
und fresh water in plenty, so one of the
st of their trials was at an end.

explorers found that they were still
miles north of Godthaab Fiord, so they
ha o work southwards, tending all the while
towards the coast, where they knew they
would have no difficulty in collecting material
with which they could build a boat of some

kind in which to complete their journey
to the nearest settlement.

It was decided tha· Nansen and Sverdrup
should go on as an a vance guard, and that
the res of the party should follow as quickly
as possible with the sledges.   They made but
slow progress, howe ·, the ice being so
rough t it for a great part of the way the
men found themselves obliged to carry the
sledges bodily. But th   pressed forward
ravely, for they realized that it was necessary
·n now for every man to exert himself
  the utmost if they were to avoid the
pleasant necessity of spending a long and
dreary winter in this inhospitable part of
Greenland.

Having at length reached the foot of the
last ice slope they decided to abandon the
sledges, which were of no further practical
use, with all the stores they   ·· '
do without. Their absolute ·
made up into bundles,
shouldered as they set out on ι.
over the rough and boggy
lay between them and the   \
they camped beside a fr   ικ·',
gathered round a blazing ι ιther
revelling in its warmth, and enjoying ·
cheerful glow to which for weeks the . had
been strangers.

The following morning Nansen was disappointed to find that the map on which ιe

had been relying was not correct, and that a journey of twelve miles still lay between the travellers and their goal. The ground was so rough and the men so heavily laden that this was too great a distance to be covered in one day, and so one more night in camp was necessary.

The next day Balto, going off alone after dinner to reconnoitre, was seen after a while high up on a mountain side vigorously waving his cap, and evidently greatly excited. When he returned he reported that the fiord was in sight at last, and that the upper end of it was covered with ice. At once it was decided to cross the mountain ; but on reaching the summit Balto's ice was seen to be sand. Far down the mountain side the party pitched their camp ; and theirs was the joy that night of feeling that the stupendous task they had undertaken was now practically accomplished.

But, though they had now crossed the mighty and hitherto unconquered Inland Ice, they had not yet reached Godthaab ; and the best and quickest way of getting there was now the most pressing problem. The sea route was decided upon as the most feasible, and Nansen and Sverdrup agreed to go on and open up communication, while the rest of the party returned for the sledges and stores.

After infinite trouble a boat was built with

willow trees growing close at hand—in itself a notable achievement when it is remembered that it was accomplished with scarcely a single tool suitable for the purpose, and Nansen and his companion prepared to commence their journey. The voyage proved to be an exceedingly trying one, but it was over at last, and the two travellers arrived in safety at the Moravian settlement of Ny Herrnhut, near Godthaab. Here their appearance caused an immense amount of excitement ; but amid the general din and hubbub one young man, a European, approached Nansen, and proclaiming himself a Dane, was soon in eager conversation with the brave and daring Norwegian. He proved to be assistant superintendent of the " coloni " of Godthaab, and was able to inform Nansen as to the possibility of getting a ship to convey his party home.

It turned out that only one vessel still remained in harbour of Ivigtut—the *Fox*, which long before had become famous in connection with the search for Franklin. The *Fox* was due to sail about the middle of October ; but Ivigtut was some three hundred miles south of Godthaab, and there was no possibility of getting there in time unless her captain would agree to wait for the travellers, or else come to Godthaab to fetch them.

A message was sent to the captain and in

due time his reply was received to the effect that he did not feel justified, so late in the season, in returning to Godthaab. However, it was comforting to know that at any rate the *Fox* would carry home reassuring news to the relatives and friends of the explorers, who had become most anxious as to their safety.

Meanwhile boats were sent from Godthaab to meet Dietrichson and the other members of the party who had turned back to fetch the sledges and stores. They had had a difficult and trying time owing to the rotten condition of the ice on the many lakes that had to be crossed—their troubles culminating in an accident to Dietrichson, who, to save time, tried to cross a lake which the others had skirted, and in the middle of it fell through the ice. The mishap might easily have proved fatal, and he only saved himself by swimming and scrambling in the icy water till he reached the opposite bank.

The arrival of the relief expedition was naturally hailed with delight by Dietrichson and the rest; and a few days later they rejoined their leader without further mishap, and settled down with him to spend the winter amongst the kindly, hospitable Greenlanders, who did their utmost to relieve the tedium of their enforced visit, and to make the sojourn of their guests as pleasant as possible.

In the following spring a ship arrived on which the travellers embarked for home. They reached Christiania on May 30th, and Nansen was deservedly accorded a splendid welcome. He had achieved a notable victory, for he had traversed from east to west a land hitherto unknown, and had solved once for all the mystery of the Inland Ice of Greenland.

CHAPTER XIV.

NANSEN had by no means reached the goal of his ambition when he had succeeded in crossing Greenland. At the time when he was preparing for that great enterprise, a friend had suggested that some day he must try and reach the North Pole. " I mean to," was his instant reply, given in such a way as to leave no doubt that his determination to attempt the achievement of this crowning triumph was already fixed.

After his return from his famous journey across the Inland Ice, Nansen spent about four years in writing the story of that great undertaking, in lecturing before learned societies, in discharging the duties of curator of a scientific museum connected with Christiania University, and in preparing the Polar expedition which he had already determined to undertake. He had given a great deal of thought to the project, and he intended to proceed on lines entirely different from those adopted by his predecessors. They had, for instance, tried to keep out of the ice as long as possible, bending all their energies to the task of finding open water, so that they might sail, during the few brief weeks of Arctic summer, towards the Pole.   Nansen's plan was deliberately to seek the ice, and allow his vessel to become locked in it, and to drift northward with the ice that imprisoned him. To do this, he had a vessel specially constructed to withstand ice pressure —one that, instead of being crushed by the floes, would probably be lifted up as they pressed hard upon her.

The special preparations for the expedition occupied three years.   At the end of that time his plans were completed, his ship was ready—provisioned with food carefully selected by the explorer and sufficient in quantity to last for several years, and his crew of twelve was chosen ;   and   on   June 24th, 1893, he set sail in his vessel, the *Fram*.

Steadily, and without adventure beyond that occasioned by hunting walruses and bears, the sturdy little *Fram* proceeded on her way, until her daring commander accomplished the purpose he had in view, and found himself in the position which all previous explorers had regarded as a calamity to be avoided at all costs—a prisoner in the grip of the ice, with no possibility of escape for months to come.

Held fast in her icy bed the *Fram* drifted

slowly; but after some months Nansen found his progress was disappointingly slow, and moreover he was not proceeding all the time in the right direction. He came to the conclusion that he could get on more quickly by travelling over the ice than by drifting with it, and so he resolved to leave the *Fram*, and accompanied by only one member of his party, journey northwards by sledge.

Elaborate preparations were made for this dangerous expedition. An abundant supply of provisions for the travellers and their dogs had to be taken; and besides scientific instruments, many pairs of snow-shoes, sleeping bag, tent, cooking stove, and oil for fuel, two kayaks were added to the equipment for crossing " lanes " of water in the ice, and for coasting along the shore. Lieutenant Johansen was selected as the leader's companion for the adventurous journey; and when all was ready they bade farewell to their comrades on the *Fram*, and set off. They had three sledges with a team of nine dogs for each; and the weight on each sledge was about four hundredweight. Their stock of food was calculated to last about one hundred days, but they hoped to supplement this by their prowess as hunters.

From the first their way was beset with difficulties, and of these the cracks and lanes in the ice were not the least. On one occasion the dogs attached to the leading sledge all

A FALL INTO A CREVASSE.

fell into a crack; and the sledge following met with a similar mishap and had to be unloaded before it could be hauled out. An even worse mishap occurred when a crack suddenly appeared in the ice, separating the leading sledge from the two that followed it, leaving Nansen on one side with one sledge, and Johansen on the other side with two sledges, and the tent and sleeping bag. The prospect for Nansen was alarming; for without the protection of the tent and the bag he could not possibly have survived the night. It was only after a long walk that Nansen reached the end of the crack, and was able to rejoin his companion, who meanwhile had fallen into the water and got his legs wet. His lower extremities were encased in ice by the time Nansen reached him; and some idea of the misery he endured may be imagined when it is stated that his frozen garments had to be kept on the body while they were thawed and dried again.

So great were their difficulties, that they considered seven miles a good day's journey; and it soon became evident that at this rate of progress they could not get far enough to serve any useful purpose before the winter set in. It was moreover imperative for their own safety that they must reach land ere the summer ended; and so, very reluctantly, all hope of reaching the North Pole was abandoned, and they turned southward on April

9th, after having reached a point some two hundred miles farther north than that attained by any previous Arctic explorer.

The journey southward proved to be even more difficult and arduous than that to the north. Their way was impeded by tremendous snowstorms, in which it was impossible to see their course. Time after time they had to stop on account of thick mists, in which they dared not move for fear of falling through a hole or crack in the ice. To make up for these delays they sometimes travelled, when the weather conditions were favourable, for twenty-four hours at a stretch ; but these forced marches were very exhausting ; and once they were so tired that they slept for twenty-two consecutive hours.

For weeks they struggled on, until at last scarcity of food and fuel began to cause them keen anxiety ; but signs of life became more frequent as they progressed steadily southward ; and their relief was great when, after enduring many days of ravenous hunger, they shot a seal. This joy however, was not unattended by misfortune, for Nansen, in his eagerness to capture the animal, let go one of the sledges which had been hauled half way up the ice, and allowed it to slip back on to one of the kayaks, in which they had packed all their store of bread. The kayak heeled over, and the bread was thoroughly soaked, and had to be dried in a frying pan over the lamp. This operation took several days, and the flavour of the bread was not improved by the process ; but when men are desperately hungry they take little heed of such trifles as that.

At the end of one of their long marches they reached a lane which could only be crossed in their kayaks. Nansen was busy with the boats at the edge of the ice when a sudden shout caused him to turn quickly. Johansen was on his back in the snow grasping a big bear by the throat! Nansen's gun was in one of the kayaks ; and in reaching for it he caused the boat to slip down into the water. It was no easy matter to haul it back ; and as he was doing so Nansen heard his companion remark quietly, " You must look sharp if you want to be in time." Nansen was already doing his utmost, and with another mighty tug he hauled the kayak into safety. Seizing his gun he fired at the bear, fortunately killing it, and so saved his friend. Johansen had a marvellous escape, for the bear had only slightly injured one of his hands.

At length the explorers reached the edge of the vast Polar ice field over which they had been travelling for five months, and a belt of open sea was all that lay between them and the glacier-covered land which they had so long desired to reach. At once they made preparations for continuing their journey by water. All their dogs except two had long since been sacrificed, and now, with great reluctance, these also were shot, since it was impossible to take them further.

After a short run before the wind the glacier was reached ; but they had great difficulty in finding a suitable landing place ; and for several days they had to sail or paddle along the shore ice, camping on ice loes each night, and running considerable risk from walruses that frequently attacked them.

At last they reached a spot where real land with moss and flowers was to be seen ; but even there they dared not linger, and after resting for only a day they pushed on, hoping that before the winter set in they might be able to reach ice-free water, across which they could sail to Spitzbergen, where they might find a ship to take them home. But this was not to be; and they had to face the certainty of having to spend the winter where they were.

They began their preparation for the coming months of darkness by laying in a stock of meat and blubber ; and having accomplished this their next care was to build winter quarters. This they did by digging a pit ten feet long, six feet wide, and three feet deep, on the margin of which they built snow walls three feet high ; so that the total height of this dwelling was six feet, and half of it was underground. The roof was made of driftwood and walrus hide. The only furniture of the hut was a platform of stones, which served as a sleeping shelf. The stones were covered with bear skins, but there were not sufficient to counteract the hardness of the stones, so that the explorers' bed was anything but comfortable. Their only fuel was blubber, burned in home-made lamps, which served also for light. Nansen had hoped to do a good deal of writing during that long, monotonous winter ; but he found that his hands and clothes blackened and greased the paper, so that he was obliged to abandon his literary work.

The two friends found the long, dreary weeks of darkness extremely trying, and often they thought enviously of their comrades on the *Fram*, with a whole library of books and all sorts of devices for making the time pass pleasantly. They suffered much, too, from their inability to clean either themselves or their clothing. Their garments became saturated with blubber and oil ; their faces and hands became black, and their hair and beards grew to such a length that they bore no resemblance whatever to the trim, fair haired, fair complexioned men who had left the *Fram* only a few months previously.

When they wanted to spend a really happy hour, Nansen says, they tried to imagine a great, bright, clean shop, where the walls were hung with nothing but new, clean, soft woollen things, from which they could select everything they needed. "Only to think of shirts, vests, drawers, soft and warm woollen trousers, deliciously comfortable jerseys, and then clean woollen stockings and warm felt slippers—could anything more delightful be imagined ? And then a Turkish bath. We would sit up side by side in our sleeping bag for hours at a time and talk of all these things."

But the long winter wore away at last ; and when at length the light returned the prisoners of the Arctic began to prepare for departure. They made new suits out of their blankets, and a new sleeping bag from bear skins, obtaining the necessary thread by unravelling canvas. Socks and gloves they also manufactured, and they soled their shoes with walrus hide scraped to half its thickness, and then dried over the lamp.

In anticipation of the journey which was now about to begin, they had buried what remained of the food with which they had left the *Fram* ; but when they dug it up they were disappointed to find that much of it was spoilt by damp, and only a little fish-flour, ordinary flour and biscuits were fit for use. Some of the mouldy bread, however, they used by boiling it in train-oil. This they regarded as a rare luxury, and it was kept for special occasions. The scan·y provisions obtained from the *cache* were supplemented by as much bear flesh and blubber from their larder as they could carry, and also three tin boxes filled with train-oil.

The preparations for their journey took a good deal of time, but with all the summer before them there was no particular need for hurry, and it was not until May 19th that they bade farewell to their winter quarters, in which they left suspended from the roof a cylinder containing a brief record of their expedition.

After three weeks of difficult travel they reached the edge of the ice, and were thankful to see the blue water of the open sea before them. Lashing their kayaks together they transferred their sledges to the deck of the double boat, and had a long and restful day's sail. At the end of the day they decided to go ashore, in order to get a more distant view than was possible from the deck of the kayaks. Accordingly they drew up to the ice ; and having, as they thought, securely fastened the boats with the only cable available—a strip of raw walrus-hide—they climbed to the top of a convenient hummock.

They stood there for a few minutes, looking about them, and never dreaming of danger, when, chancing to glance towards the kayaks, they were horrified to find that the boats had broken loose from their mooring, and were drifting away. The horror of the situation will be apparent when it is remembered that their two boats were not only the sole means by which these men would be able to rejoin their friends, but that they contained literally everything they possessed. They must regain those boats, or slowly perish of cold and starvation.

With a wild rush Nansen tore down to the water's edge, divesting himself of some of his clothing as he ran, and plunged into the icy sea. With bold strokes he swam towards the drifting boats. In a few moments the intense cold had so benumbed him that further progress seemed impossible ; but with the superhuman energy of a desperate man, who knows that he is fighting for his life, and that it is death to turn back, he struggled on. Looking ahead, he was greatly encouraged to find that he was slowly approaching the boats, and he redoubled his efforts.

At last, with one final despairing spurt he managed to reach the kayaks and scramble on board—in itself no easy task for a man already exhausted as he was. Then, standing in the icy wind, shivering and half frozen, he began with weak, uncertain strokes to paddle the double canoe shorewards where Johansen awaited him in an agony of doubt as to whether his leader's strength would hold out until he reached him. At length he reached the floe, when Johansen stretched out eager hands to help him to land ; and then, having put on the few dry garments he possessed, he crawled into his sleeping bag, where he soon fell asleep. A few hours later he was quite ready for the hot soup that Johansen had prepared for him, and he appeared to be none the worse for his perilous experience.

But the explorers were not yet out of danger— a fact of which they had disagreeable proof two days later, when a belligerent walrus thrust his tusks clean through the bottom of one of the kayaks, and made a deliberate attempt to upset what he evidently believed to be some strange monster of the deep. The attack was entirely unprovoked, and Nansen, who had fortunately just escaped being impaled on those vicious tusks, grasped his paddle and made such a spirited defence that the walrus, doubtless thinking discretion the better part of valour, gracefully retired from the conflict and left Nansen to run his damaged kayak ashore just in time to prevent it sinking, but not soon enough to prevent practically the whole of its contents from being soaked by the inrushing water.

The next day was spent by the explorers in repairing their boat, and in drying the wet goods ; and after a night's rest preparations were set forward for resuming the journey. Nansen was in the midst of cooking a somewhat belated breakfast when a sound to which he had long been a stranger startled him. He listened intently, and soon heard it again. The unmistakable bark of a dog. Obviously the dog's master could not be far away. With a joyful cry Nansen awoke his still sleeping companion, and after a hurried meal rushed off on his ski in the direction whence that welcome sound had come. As he went he heard another bark and then a shout ; and presently, looking up, he saw a man coming towards him. The newcomer proved to be Mr. F. G. Jackson, of the Jackson-Harmsworth expedition ; and soon the two explorers were heartily greeting each other. Johansen was quickly informed of the happy meeting ; and when he too had joined Mr. Jackson's party, the adventures of these two heroes of the Arctic were at an end, and subsequently on board the *Windward* they were brought back to Norway in safety.

Meanwhile, thanks to the careful observance of instructions left by Nansen, the *Fram* had successfully overcome all the dangers to which she was exposed ; and ultimately the reunited members of the expedition reached Christiania, where they received at the hands of their countrymen the honours they so richly deserved.

CHAPTER XV.

THE CONQUEST OF THE NORTH POLE.

THE expedition of Nansen across the Inland Ice had conclusively proved that in the interior of Greenland there was no habitable land. But there still remained another mystery to be solved. It was not yet known whether Greenland was part of the great Polar continent, or whether it was merely an island; and the settlement of this point presented a problem which had a peculiar fascination for more than one explorer.

Amongst the many men who had studied this question was Lieutenant Peary, an officer of the United States Navy. He had already some experience of Greenland, for in 1886 he had been on the Inland Ice; and it had ever since been his ambition to traverse some hitherto unexplored portion of the country. His naval duties for some years prevented this; but at last an opportunity presented itself, and he quickly made up his mind that he would endeavour to explore the north coast with a view to a final settlement of the problem of Greenland's actual geographical character.

The only practicable way of starting on such an expedition as Peary had in view was by taking ship to the most northerly point attainable and thence proceeding on ski or snow-shoes over the ice-cap ; and as it is useless to attempt a journey of any length across the ice unless a start is made in the early summer, it would be necessary to reach the starting place at the beginning of winter, and spend the whole of the winter season there, in readiness to set out across the ice on the very first possible day.

This, of course, involved very heavy expense ; for it necessitated provisioning the expedition for a long period, and a substantial house would also have to be built to serve as winter quarters. The Government could give the explorer no financial help, though he was freely granted leave for his undertaking ; and the necessary funds came from his own pocket and from private sources. The Academy of Natural Sciences of Philadelphia generously provided a steamer to convey Peary and his party to the point from which the journey across the ice was to be made, and he was landed there with all the stores necessary for an absence which he calculated would last about eighteen months. His companions were six in number, and included Mrs. Peary, who most courageously resolved to accompany her husband ; and on June 6th, 1891, the party set out in the whaler *Kite*—a small but exceedingly strong vessel which had been specially built for Arctic service.

The sea journey was not without its dangers and difficulties ; and the explorers had not long been afloat before they found themselves in the midst of a thick fog and surrounded by an ice pack. A strong breeze relieved them of this discomfort, but the breeze rapidly strengthened to a gale, and the little ship was knocked about considerably. She kept sturdily on her way, however, until she came within the determined grip of the ice, and then her progress was slow indeed. Sometimes for days together it was impossible for the ship to move at all, and these long stoppages were very trying. Peary, too, met with an unfortunate accident on the ship, and injured himself so seriously that some of the party suggested the expedition should be abandoned ; but their leader, reminding them he had the whole winter before him in which to recover, pluckily decided to go on.

As the vessel proceeded northward the difficulties of steering a course through the masses of ice became greater ; and several times great floes were blown up with gunpowder, which was placed in bottles to which safety fuses were attached. These curious cartridges were fixed in holes drilled in the ice, and they served their purpose admirably ; and at last, after almost interminable delays, the *Kite* reached Whale Sound, on the shores of which it had been agreed the party should be landed and left for the winter.

It was on the north shore of the sound that Peary wished to make his camp, and while the captain of the *Kite* was searching for a suitable landing-place, he saw through his telescope the skin tents and earth huts of what proved to be an Esquimaux village— the most northerly settlement in the world. The village was very small, but interesting ; and as the natives lived so far out of the track of even the whaling ships that they had never seen white men before, the interest of the visitors and the visited was mutual.

The neighbourhood of the village, however, afforded no suitable place for winter quarters, so after a brief stay the explorers steamed away, and finally a camping ground was selected on the south shore of McCormick Bay, beneath a towering cliff of sandstone.

On July 25th the landing was effected and on the following day the work of house building was put in hand, the crippled leader being accommodated in a tent, from which he directed operations ; while Mrs. Peary found plenty to do in tending her husband and supervising the landing and disposal of the stores.

Everybody worked with a will ; and in a

Photo.] SEAL HUNTERS. [Underwood & Underwood.

very few days the stores were all on shore, and the building operations so far advanced that the *Kite* was at liberty to depart on her homeward voyage ; and with a final salute from her guns she steamed away and left Peary and his companions to their own devices.

By the time the house was finished Mr. Peary was able to get about with the aid of crutches, and he began to organize hunting expeditions—in which he could of course take no active part, but which were hugely enjoyed by the others. He also induced an Esquimaux family from a neighbouring island to come and take up their abode near the camp. Ikwa, the father of the family, proved most useful in teaching the explorers the mysteries of Arctic hunting, and Mané, his wife, proved an adept in the manufacture of fur clothing. They were, however, as uncouth and unclean as the rest of their race ; and on one occasion Ikwa took serious offence because he was not allowed to bring to camp a seal which he found and which had been so long dead that its odour was simply insupportable. To Ikwa there was nothing but a sweet smelling savour about it which was altogether delightful ; and he was greatly annoyed when Mr. Peary compelled him to abandon what he and Mané considered a rare delicacy !

With the end of September came winter in real earnest, and the hunting trips and other out-door activities had to be considerably

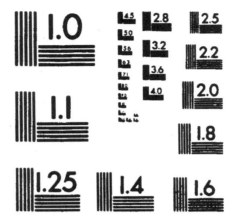

MICROCOPY RESOLUTION TEST CHART
NATIONAL BUREAU OF STANDARDS
STANDARD REFERENCE MATERIAL 1010a
(ANSI and ISO TEST CHART No. 2)

curtailed; but life indoors was not without its attractions, and the house had been made so cosy and comfortable that the party contrived to enjoy themselves very considerably. Tailoring was the principal occupation, and with the help of the Esquimaux a good many serviceable, if not exactly handsome, fur garments were made. Then came Christmas —a right merry time for everyone—and so winter passed, and the time approached for commencing the task which was the real object of the expedition.

About the middle of April Mr. Peary— whose health was now perfectly restored— set out with Mrs. Peary on a week's sledging excursion, their object being to explore Inglefield Gulf. They took with them an Esquimaux, whose unpronounceable name they shortened to Kyo, and on a sledge drawn by six dogs they set forth. Their first day's journey ended in a terrific snowstorm, and Mr. Peary decided to accept an offer of hospitality from a kindly Esquimaux who invited them to stay the night in his " igloo," or hut. It was a dark, dirty, evil smelling place, entrance to which was only to be had by crawling on hands and knees through a low passage. In this undignified fashion Mrs. Peary as well as her husband was obliged to enter the hovel, where they spent the night in extreme discomfort.

To their great relief they found next morn-

ing the storm had sufficiently abated for them
to resume their journey ; and the next night
they resolved to build a snow hut for themselves, rather than accept native hospitality.
But the hut, though clean, was cold ; and
they decided thereafter to sleep in the open
air. The next camping place was a sheltered
spot on the shore ; but alas ! in their ignor-
ance the explorers had established themselves
within reach of the incoming tide ; and they
were rudely awakened by a tumbling wave
that first soaked Mr. Peary's clothes, which
were serving as a pillow, and then drenched
him as he lay slumbering in his sleeping bag.
The unexpected cold bath roused him effectu-
ally, and fortunately in time to rescue
Mrs. Peary before the water reached her ;
but the experience was a trying one !

The next day the Pearys turned homeward again, and reached camp without further
mishap. Their trial trip had been on the whole
very successful ; for they had traversed
hitherto unknown ground, and had done some
good and useful geographical work ; while
their experience had given them courage and
had convinced them that there was every
prospect of accomplishing their great journey
successfully.

Preparations for this journey now commenced in real earnest. The Esquimaux
watched the proceedings with interest and
gave what help they could ; but they were

firmly convinced that the white men would never succeed in their undertaking. The ice-cap was the home of a terrible demon, whom they called Korkoya, and who would never permit any one to invade his domain. He devoured all who ventured within his borders, and the fate of these misguided white people was therefore certain !

But the white people were quite cheerfully prepared to take the risk, and they preserved their light-heartedness even when they found that owing to the rough and broken condition of the ice their sledges would be of little use, and that all their equipment would have to be carried on their own backs for a great part of the way. It had been decided that Mrs. Peary should remain at head quarters with Verhoeff, the mineralogist to the expedition ; while the others—Dr. Cook, Gibson, Astrup, and Henson—accompanied the leader.

From the first, difficulties beset these adventurers into the unknown. They found dog-driving by no means easy work, and it was some days before the animals settled down to their task and submitted to be driven by men whom they knew quite well to be unaccustomed to them and their ways. It was distinctly trying when the dogs, for instance, broke away from the sledge or tangled themselves in their harness ; and it needed all the patience and ingenuity of their drivers to subdue them and keep them in order.

Two days after they had started they encountered a terrible storm. The gale was so strong that sharp fragments of ice were picked up by the wind and flung in the faces of the men, making progress so difficult and painful that after a while a halt was called and they built snow huts in which to take shelter. The huts, however, were so piercingly cold that they were compelled to abandon them, and when they did so they found the sledges were almost buried in the snow and the dogs had taken advantage of their brief spell of liberty and leisure to chew up their harness !

The appetite of dogs in the Arctic is truly prodigious, and sometimes it has quite disconcerting results. Sir F. L. McClintock tells of an amusing incident that happened to one of the men who accompanied him on his expedition in search of Sir John Franklin. "The dogs," he says, "are continually on the look-out for anything eatable. Hobson made one very happy without intending it. He meant only to give him a kick ; but his slipper, being down at heel, flew off, and was instantly snapped up and carried off in triumph by this lucky dog, who demolished it at his leisure away amongst the hummocks."

Peary and his companions bravely struggled

on until the Humboldt Glacier was reached. Here the leader decided that all save one of the men and himself should return ; and he left it to his followers to settle amongst themselves who should accompany him on the remainder of the journey. They were all so eager, however, to go on with Peary, that he was after all obliged to settle the matter himself ; and he finally decided to take Astrup, as being more experienced than the others in the use of ski, and therefore probably more likely to be helpful.

Peary selected thirteen of the dogs and three sledges. The loads were re-arranged, the sledges overhauled and thoroughly repaired, and then with mutual good-byes and good wishes the party separated, Peary and Astrup continuing the journey alone while the others turned back towards headquarters, which they reached without mishap.

Peary and his companion took a north-easterly course over the ice cap ; and after a week of hard travelling found themselves above Petermann Fjord. After this stage of their journey the weather, which had hitherto been fairly favourable, changed for the worse and travel became much more difficult owing to frequent fissures and crevasses in the ice, which it was almost impossible for the dogs to negotiate. Then another storm overtook the travellers and caused them intense suffering, their only shelter being a three sided erection of blocks of frozen snow, arranged by Astrup, and roofed with a slight sail. Here, exposed to biting wind and piercing cold, and with no possibility of warmth beyond that afforded by a small and entirely inadequate spirit stove, the men were obliged to remain for two whole days.

When at length the storm ceased and progress was again possible, Peary found that it would be necessary to strike inland instead of continuing to follow the coast line, in order to get clear of the rough and broken ice which had hitherto greatly impeded them. This involved a good deal of difficult climbing; and before it was accomplished the best of the dogs sprained his foot so badly that he had to be shot. Then in dragging the sledges up hill the largest of them had been so badly damaged that a whole day was spent in repairing it. The labour, too, of hauling the sledges up the icy slopes was so great that they were obliged to cast away everything but the barest necessities in order to lighten their load as much as possible.

The troubles of the travellers increased as they went onward, but they persevered until they came in sight of a range of mountains to the eastward, while before them lay a stretch of country barren and stony, but, like the mountains in the distance, quite free from ice or snow. The question in the minds of the explorers was, had they at last crossed the great Greenland ice-cap and was that range of distant mountains the boundary of the country, with the sea beyond?

There was only one possible way to settle the matter, and Peary adopted it without hesitation. Leaving Astrup in charge of the dogs and the sledges, he set out alone for the mountains, which were apparently about five miles off, intending to see for himself what lay beyond. He found the way difficult and painful, for the ground was covered with splinters of stone so sharp that they cut his boots. But he went doggedly on, until not only five but fifteen miles had been covered. And still he had not reached the mountains. At length, with torn boots and bleeding feet the weary man had to own himself beaten for the time, and reluctantly he turned back, reaching camp twenty-four hours after he had set out, to the great relief of Astrup, who had begun to think his leader was lost.

After a good meal and a sleep the indomitable Peary started again; but this time Astrup went with him. They took the dogs also and food enough to last them five days. They tried another route for the new journey, but it proved if anything worse than the first, and they had great difficulty in making their way through snowy sludge and amongst needle pointed stones. But they were determined not to be overcome, and at last the mountains were reached and climbed. Then the two weary men were rewarded with a sight which repaid them for all their toil. Below them lay the sea, behind them was the Inland Ice over which they had travelled so painfully; and they realized that they had now accomplished the task they had set themselves, for they had proved C   d's insularity.

They   airn, in which they deposited a record   achievement, and they unfurled the   flag of their country which had been presented to the expedition by the Academy, and planted it on the top of the cairn. They occupied themselves for a day or two in making observations and taking photographs, and then the homeward journey was begun. This was accomplished in safety, and at last the two brave men reached McCormack Bay, to be joyfully welcomed by their friends, having won a triumph which worthily holds a high place in the records of endeavour and achievement in the far north.

But a greater triumph still was in store for the intrepid Peary. The expedition which had resulted so brilliantly made him the more determined not to accept defeat in the supreme aim he had in view, namely the conquest of the Pole itself. During the twenty-three years from 1886 to 1909 he spent fifteen summers and eight winters within the Arctic circle. If any man ever deserved success it was

Commander Peary, without doubt the most daring and persevering of all Arctic explorers.

Eight times in all this dauntless man ventured into the far north. His eighth voyage —the one that brought him his great, final triumph—was begun on July 6th, 1908. With a carefully chosen company he left New York on that day in the *Roosevelt* for the Arctic regions. Peary's intention this time was to endeavour to reach the Pole by sledge from Cape Columbia ; and on February 22nd, 1909, he left the ship at the head of an expedition consisting of seven men of his own party, fifty-nine Esquimaux, one hundred and forty dogs and twenty-three sledges. After a series of marches truly remarkable for their length, and for the dogged endurance and perseverance which they demanded from all concerned, a spot was reached on April 6th which careful observation proved to be within three geographical miles of the Pole.

For thirty hours Peary and the Esquimaux who accompanied him remained at this bleak and frozen extremity of the earth, making records and taking photographs.

On the following day they left and returned to the *Roosevelt* with the astounding news that the goal towards which men had vainly struggled for four long centuries had been reached at last. Without a single adventure worth recording—in a manner that by comparison with the efforts of previous

explorers seems almost tame and common-
place—the great conquest was at last completed ; and to Commander Peary belongs the
honour of having been the first of the human
race to attain that goal for which so many
other brave men had sacrificed their lives—
the North Pole itself.

CHAPTER XVI.

POLAR EXPLORATION IN SOUTHERN SEAS.

UNTIL within comparatively recent times Antarctic exploration has not attracted anything like the attention that for hundreds of years has been given by British explorers to the northern Polar regions. The principal reason for this lies in the fact of our tremendous distance from the South Pole. We are separated by seven thousand miles from the Antarctic Circle; and though voyages of discovery in that region have from time to time been undertaken—voyages that have added considerably to the world's knowledge, besides proving of the greatest importance to the British Empire—they have never roused the general interest and enthusiasm that have usually resulted from similar expeditions in the north.

But during the past few years the importance of a thorough exploration of the far south has been realized as never before. Expeditions h: been organized, and men as brave as any who ever risked their lives in northern regions have undertaken to try and penetrate the southern ice field, even to the South Pole itself. In this endeavour they have suffered greatly and have experienced many stirring adventures and thrilling escapes; and in the following pages are recounted briefly some of the more noteworthy attempts and achievements of these heroes of the southern seas.

First it may be of interest to recall that the earliest English explorer to venture into far southern regions was Sir Francis Drake, who in 1578 set out "to seek that strait in which the vulgar believe not, but the reality of which is confirmed by many cosmographers." He found the strait—Magellan—and sailed through it into the Pacific, reaching in the course of his voyage the most southerly point yet attained, though he was still nine degrees north of the Antarctic Circle.

Many subsequent voyages to the southern polar seas were undertaken by men of various nationalities; but nothing of great importance was achieved until the famous undertaking of Captain Cook, who was the first navigator to solve finally the problem of the existence of a great southern continent. During his voyage he entered the Antarctic Circle on January 17th, 1773; and to him and his ship's company belongs the honour of having been the first human beings to do this.

Cook's voyage, however, was not for the purpose of discovering the South Pole, and he turned his ship northward again. A year later he found himself once more within the Antarctic Circle, and this time he penetrated farther within it, reaching, on January 30th, 1774, the most southerly point until then attained by man. The brave sailor thus describes this epoch-marking event in the world's history.

"On the 30th, at four o'clock in the morning, we perceived the clouds, over the horizon, to the south, to be of an unusual snow-white brightness, which we knew announced our approach to field-ice. Soon after it was seen from the topmast head, and at eight o'clock we were close to its edge. It extended east and west far beyond the reach of our sight. In the situation we were in, just the southern half of our horizon was illuminated by the rays of light reflected from the ice to a considerable height. Ninety-seven ice hills were distinctly seen within the field, besides those on the outside—many of them very large, and looking like a ridge of mountains rising one above another till they were lost in the clouds.

"The outer or northern edge of this immense field was composed of loose or broken ice close packed together, so that it was not possible for anything to enter it. This was about a mile broad, within which was solid ice in one continued, compact body. It was rather low and flat (except the hills) but seemed to increase in height as you traced it to the south, in which direction it extended beyond our sight. Such mountains of ice as these, I think, were never seen in the Greenland Seas, at least not that I ever heard or read of, so that we cannot draw a comparison between the ice here and there. It must be allowed that these prodigious ice mountains must add such additional weight to the ice-fields which enclose them as cannot but make a great difference between the navigating this icy sea and that of Greenland.

" I will not say that it was impossible anywhere to get farther to the south ; but attempting it would have been a dangerous and rash enterprise, and one which, I believe, no man in my situation would have thought of. It was, indeed, my opinion, as well as the opinion of most on board, that this ice extended quite to the pole, or perhaps joined on some land to which it had been fixed from the earliest time, and that it is here, that is to the south of this parallel, where all the ice we find scattered up and down to the north is first formed and afterwards broken off by gales of wind or other causes, and brought to the north by the currents, which are always found to set in that direction in high latitudes.

" As we drew near this ice some penguins

were heard, but none seen ; and but few other birds, or anything that could induce us to think any land was near. And yet I think that there must be some to the south behind this ice ; but if there is, it can afford no better retreat for birds or any other animals than the ice itself, with which it must be wholly covered. I, who had ambition to go not only farther than anyone had been before, but as far as it was possible for man to go, was not sorry to meet with this interruption, as it in some measure relieved us, at least shortened the dangers and hardships insepar-able from the navigation of the southern polar regions. Since, therefore, we could not proceed one inch farther to the south, no other reason need be assigned for my tacking and standing back to the north."

It is probable, however, that another reason lay in the fact that Cook could no longer stand the anxiety and exposure necessary to the navigation of a ship in such bleak and dangerous waters ; and that he was physically unable to endure any longer the diet of ancient salt meat and rotten biscuit half devoured by cockroaches which was the only food the ship now afforded. Indeed, shortly after he had turned the *Resolution* northwards he was attacked with what he termed " bilious colic," which nearly cost him his life.

Cook's expedition lasted three years, for it was not until July 30th, 1775, that his worn and weather-beaten vessel dropped anchor at Spithead, after one of the longest, most adventurous and most successful voyages at that time of record. His own estimate of his achievements was most modest ; and he seemed proudest of the fact that through careful attention to diet, and insistence upon the most scrupulous cleanliness, he had been enabled to preserve the health of his crew. So far as Antarctic exploration was concerned, he declared his belief that no man would ever succeed in penetrating farther south than he had done, and that the icy barrier blocking the way to the South Pole would never be broken.

For nearly fifty years after Cook's return his countrymen seem to have accepted as final his statement as to the impossibility of reaching the South Pole. Then came the announcement of an American expedition ; and this called forth in 1837 an appeal to British patriotism which found expression in a remarkable letter to the President and Council of the Royal Geographical Society on the subject of Antarctic Discovery. The letter, which was signed A. Z., contained the following impassioned words : "Oh! let it not be said that more than half a century elapsed since our immortal countryman Cook sacrificed his life in the cause of discovery, and that no steps were taken to follow up the glorious track in which he led the way —that all within the Polar circle still remains a blank on our charts; nay, infinitely more to our disgrace, that we, who date a thousand years of naval supremacy, allowed a nation but of yesterday, albeit gigantic in her infancy, to snatch from us our birthright on the ocean, and to pluck the laurels that have been planted and watered by the toils of our seamen.''

The answer to this appeal was the British Antarctic Expedition, fitted out by the Admiralty in accordance with the plan submitted by the British Association and approved by the Royal Society. The command of this expedition was given to Captain James Clarke Ross, of whose ability as an Arctic explorer the reader of this volume is already aware. Of all men, he was without doubt the best fitted, by experience and by temperament, to take charge of such an expedition, and the result proved the wisdom of those who entrusted the difficult and arduous task of directing such an enterprise to his capable hands.

Two vessels were set apart for the expedition—the *Erebus* and the *Terror*. Ross was appointed to the command of the first, and his old shipmate, Commander Francis R. M. Crozier, was placed in charge of the second. On September 25th, 1839, the two vessels set sail, and Ross recorded that he found it "not easy to describe the joy and light-heartedness" of being at last fairly launched on an enterprise which he had long desired to undertake. After a long and stormy voyage the Antarctic Circle was reached, and "joy and satisfaction beamed on every face as the crews knew that nothing now lay between them and their goal."

Ross spent the long period of 145 days within the circle, and then returned to Van Dieman's Land with every member of his crews in good health and with a splendid record of discovery. Three months were spent in rest for the crews and in the refitting of the ships; and then the vessels once more sailed south-ward, reaching the Antarctic Circle again at the end of the year.

The last few days of the year were marked by embarrassing fogs and light winds, so that progress became exasperatingly slow, and Christmas Day found the ships "closely beset in the pack, near to a chain of eleven bergs of the barrier kind, and in a thick fog the greater part of the day, with by no means a cheering prospect before us; we nevertheless managed to do justice to the good old English fare which we had taken care to preserve for the occasion." The New Year, too, was welcomed with great merriment and with all the noise that the crews could contrive to make, the festivities culminating in a grand fancy ball of a novel and original character, in which all the officers took part, adding much to the fun and merriment, which everybody seemed greatly to enjoy. "Indeed," says Ross, " if our friends in England could have witnessed the scene they would have thought, what I am sure was truly the case, that we were a very happy party." It was well that they made the most of their opportunity of enjoyment, for there were days ahead of them when they would need all the remembrance of their fun and light-heartedness to help them through hours of hard toil and keen anxiety.

For some days during January the ships were confined in a " hole " in the ice, about half a mile in diameter; and on the 17th the barometer warned them of an approaching gale. On the following day the storm broke while the two vessels were slowly forging through a thick fog, kept apart by a heavy ice floe which they towed between them for the purpose. The wind veered round to the north-west at midnight; and what happened afterwards is best described in Ross's own words.

"All our hawsers breaking in succession we made sail on the ships and kept company during the thick fog by firing guns, and by means of the usual signals. Under the shelter of a berg of nearly a mile in diameter, we dodged about during the whole day, waiting for clear weather, that we might select the best leads through the dispersing pack ; but at 9 p.m. the wind suddenly freshened to a violent gale to the northward, compelling us to reduce our sails to a close reefed main-top-sail and storm-stay-sails. The sea quickly rising to a fearful height, breaking over the loftiest bergs, we were unable any longer to hold our ground, but were driven into the heavy pack under our lee.

" Soon after midnight our ships were involved in an ocean of rolling fragments of ice, hard as floating rocks of granite, which were dashed against them by the waves with so much violence that their masts quivered as if they would fall at every successive blow ; and the destruction of the ships seemed inevitable from the tremendous shocks they received.

" By backing and filling the sails, we endeavoured to avoid collision with the larger masses ; but this was not always possible. In the early part of the storm the rudder of the *Erebus* was so much damaged as to be no longer of any use ; and about the same time I was informed by signal that the *Terror's* was completely destroyed, and nearly torn away from the stern-post. We had hoped that as we drifted deeper into the pack we should get beyond the reach of the tempest ; but in this we were mistaken. Hour passed away after hour without the least mitigation of the awful circumstances in which we were placed. Indeed there seemed but little probability of our ships holding together much longer, so frequent and violent were the shocks they sustained.

" The loud, crashing noise of the straining and working of the timbers and decks, as she was driven against some of the heavier pieces, which all the activity and exertions of our people could not prevent, was sufficient to fill the stoutest heart, that was not supported by trust in Him who controls all events, with dismay; and I should commit an act of injustice to my companions if I did not express my admiration of their conduct on this trying occasion. Throughout a period of twenty-eight hours, during any one of which there appeared to be very little hope that we should live to see another, the coolness, steady obedience and untiring exertions of each individual were in every way worthy of British seamen.

" The storm gained its height at 2 p.m. when the barometer stood at 28.40 inches and after that time began to rise. Although we had been forced many miles deeper into the pack we could not perceive that the swell had at all subsided, our ship still rolling and groaning amidst the heavy fragments of crushing bergs, over which the ocean rolled its mountainous waves, throwing huge masses one upon another, and then again burying them deep beneath the foaming waters, dashing and grinding them together with fearful violence. The awful grandeur of such a scene can neither be imagined nor described, far less can the feelings of those who witnessed it be understood. Each of us secured our hold, waiting the issue with resignation to the will of Him who alone could preserve us and bring us safely through this extreme danger ; watching with breathless anxiety the effect of each succeeding collision, and the vibrations of the tottering masts, expecting every moment to see them give way without our having the power to make an effort to save them.

" Although the force of the wind had somewhat diminished by 4 p.m., yet the squalls came on with unabated violence, laying the ship over on her broadside, and threatening to blow the storm-sails to pieces ; fortunately they were quite new, or they never could have withstood such terrific gusts. At this time the *Terror* was so close to us that when she rose to the top of one wave the *Erebus* was on the top of the next to leeward of her ; the deep chasm between them filled with heavy rolling masses ; and as the ship descended into the hollow between the waves the main-top-sail yard of each could be seen just level with the crest of the intervening wave, from the deck of the other. From this some idea may be formed of the height of the waves, as well as the perilous situation of our ships.

" The night now began to draw in, and cast its gloomy mantle over the appalling scene, rendering our condition if possible more hopeless and helpless than before ; but at midnight the snow, which had been falling thickly for several hours, cleared aw..y as the wind suddenly shifted to the westward, and the swell began to subside ; and although the shocks our ships still sustained were such that must have destroyed any ordinary vessel in less than five minutes, yet they were feeble compared to those to which we had been exposed, and our minds became more at ease for their ultimate safety.

" During the darkness of the night and the thick weather, we had been carried through a chain of bergs which was seen in the morning considerably to windward and which served to keep off the heavy pressure of the pack, so that we found the ice much more open, and I was enabled to make my way in one of our boats to the *Terror*, about whose condition I was most anxious, for I was aware that her damages were of a much more serious nature than those of the *Erebus*, notwithstanding the skilful and seamanlike manner in which she had been managed and by which she maintained her appointed station throughout the gale.

" I found that her rudder was completely

broken to pieces, and the fastenings to the stern-post so much strained and twisted that it would be very difficult to get the spare rudder, with which we were fortunately provided, fitted so as to be useful, and could only be done, if at all, under very favourable circumstances. The other damages she had sustained were of less consequence, and it was as great a satisfaction as it has ever since been a source of astonishment to us to find that after so many hours of constant and violent thumping, both the vessels were nearly as tight as they were before the gale. We can only ascribe this to the admirable manner in which they had been fortified for the service, and to our having their holds so stowed as to form a solid mass throughout."

When the gale had subsided another great ice-floe was captured and made fast between the two ships, and the carpenters and armourers set to work to repair the damage. This they accomplished after two days of almost incessant toil, and then, with   rails set, the vessels tried once more to for . .ead. This, however, they were unable to do. They could make no progress through the terrible ice pack which was steadily drifting northward; and after all the danger and stress through which they had passed they had the mortification of finding that they were in almost exactly the same position they had occupied three weeks previously.

In a few da s, however, the pack loosened ;
and, favouredy by a northerly gale, the ships
made good headway towards the open sea ;
and by the end of February they crossed the
Antarctic circle to the northward. The
intention of Captain Ross now was to cross
the South Pacific Ocean by the shortest route
and make for the Falkland Islands, where he
intended to spend the winter, as quickly as
possible.

For three days, in a sea clear of ice, the
vessels made excellent progress ; and then
suddenly, and almost without warning, they
were faced with a danger more terrible than
any they had yet encountered. The wind
increased to a gale, and blinding snow showers
obscured the look out. As daylight waned
the storm increased, and the appearance of
small pieces of ice indicated that there might
be bergs in the vicinity. But the risk of an
actual encounter with one of these grim terrors
of the adventurer in polar regions does not
seem to have disturbed the commander of the
expedition in the least. He had just decided
as a precautionary measure to lay to until
the morning, when the unexpected happened ;
and for one terrible hour it seemed that no
mortal power could save either of the ships
from destruction. Captain Ross thus tells
the story of that hour, probably the most
fearful in all his adventurous career.

" A large berg was seen ahead and quite

close to us ; the ship was immediately hauled
to the wind on the port tack, with the expectation of being able to weather it ; but just at
this moment the *Terror* was observed running
down upon us, under her top sails and fore-
sail ; and as it was impossible for her to clear
both the berg and the *Erebus*, collision was
inevitable. We instantly hove all aback
to diminish the violence of the shock, but
the concussion when she struck us was such
as to throw almost everyone off his feet ; our
bowsprit, fore-topmast, and other smaller
spars were carried away ; and the ships
hanging together, entangled by their rigging,
and dashing against each other with fearful
violence, were falling down upon the weather
face of the lofty berg under our lee, against
which the waves were breaking and foaming
to near the summit of its perpendicular
cliffs.

" Sometimes the *Terror* rose high above us,
almost exposing her keel to view, and again
descended as we in our turn rose to the top
of the wave, threatening to bury her beneath
us, whilst the crashing of the breaking upper-
works and boats increased the horror of the
scene. Providentially the ships gradually
forged past each other, and separated before we
drifted down amongst the foaming breakers,
and we had the gratification of seeing the
Terror clear the end of the berg, and of feeling
that she was safe. But she left us completely

disabled ; the wreck of the spars so encumbered the lower yards that we were unable to make sail, so as to get headway on the ship ; nor had we room to wear round, being by this time so close to the berg that the waves, when they struck against it, threw back their sprays into the ship.

" The only way left to us to extricate ourselves from this awful and appalling situation was by resorting to the hazardous expedient of a stern board, which nothing could justify during such a gale, and with so high a sea running, but to avert the danger which every moment threatened us of being dashed to pieces.

" The heavy rolling of the vessel, and the probability of the masts giving way each time the lower yard arms struck against the cliffs, which were towering high above our mast heads, rendered it a service of extreme danger to loose the main sail ; but no sooner was the order given than the daring spirit of the British seaman manifested itself—the men ran up the rigging with as much alacrity as on any ordinary occasion ; and although more than once driven off the yard, they after a short time succeeded in loosing the sail.

" Amidst the roar of the wind and sea it was difficult both to hear and to execute the orders that were given, so that it was three quarters of an hour before we could get the yards braced bye, and the maintack hauled on board sharp aback—an expedient that had perhaps never before been resorted to by seamen in such weather. But it had the desired effect ; the ship gathered sternway, plunging her stern into the sea, washing away the gig and quarter boats, and with her lower yard arms scraping the rugged face of the berg, we in a few minutes reached its western termination ; the undertow, as it is called, or the reaction of the water from its vertical cliffs, alone preventing us being driven to atoms against it.

" No sooner had we cleared it, than another was seen directly astern of us, against which we were running ; and the difficulty now was to get the ship's head turned and pointed fairly through between the two bergs, the breadth of the intervening space not exceeding three times her own breadth. This, however, we happily accomplished ; and in a few minutes after getting before the wind, she dashed through the narrow channel, between two perpendicular walls of ice, and the foaming breakers which stretched across it, and the next moment we were in smooth water under its lee."

The captain's modest and unemotional account of this thrilling experience leaves a good deal to the imagination of the reader ; but it is not difficult to believe the testimony of one of his colleagues who, in the course of a letter describing this incident, said : " We might go a thousand times more to the South Pole without experiencing one half the dangers we have this time."

The vessels reached Falkland Islands on April 6th without further adventure ; and repairs and refitting necessitated a stay of some three months in harbour. After one or two short exploring cruises in the neighbour-hood of Cape Horn, Captain Ross once more headed his vessels southwards. His third venture within the Antarctic circle was, however, comparatively unfruitful ; and in the spring of the following year he left the far southern seas for the last time, and set sail for home.

England was reached in September, 1843, after an absence of nearly four-and-a-half years, and Ross found that well-deserved honours were awaiting him. He was knighted, and several gold medals were presented to him ; but the reward that was dearest to him of all was in the fact that consequent on his splendid achievement in the south he was selected to command another expedition which was to be arranged by the Admiralty, having for its object the final solution of the problem of the north-west passage.

This command, however, he declined, for family reasons ; and except for his voyage to the Arctic regions five years later, when he commanded H.M.S. *Enterprise* in the search for Franklin, Ross ventured no more into polar seas.

His work was finished, and he had done it well ; and he could look back with pride upon a record which proved him a man bold and courageous, ready to dare and to do anything at the call of duty, for his country and for his fellow men.

CHAPTER XVII.

THE CONQUEST OF THE FAR SOUTH.

FOR thirty years or more after the last expedition of Captain Ross, no exploring ship sailed the southern seas. What has been called the Franklin era had dawned ; and— to the entire exclusion of the claims of the far south—popular interest was focussed upon the nearer north, first on Franklin's voyages, and subsequently on the many expeditions in search of him, which cast for the time being such a halo of romance around the Arctic regions. Indeed even after the public anxiety for the fate of Franklin had been set at rest by the final discovery of authentic records by Sir Leopold McClintock, enthusiasm for Antarctic exploration was confined to a very few.

True it is that more than one expedition was sent into Antarctic waters, but polar exploration was only an incident in the work, and not the main object of it. The *Challenger*, for instance, known to everyone through her splendid record in the field of maritime science,

Photo

CAPTAIN SCOTT AND HIS MOTOR SNOW SLEDGE.

[Topical Press Agency.

penetrated the far south, but mainly for the purpose of investigating the marine biology of the Antarctic ; and it is not greatly to the credit of a nation that prides itself on the encouragement it gives to those who seek to explore undiscovered corners of the earth, that a real, living interest in the work of Antarctic exploration was revived by men who ventured south in search of whales !

The whale fishery of the north, once a source of immense wealth, had become exhausted ; and in 1892 four vessels of a Dundee fleet of whalers were equipped for a southern voyage, the owners hoping that a profitable whaling industry might be established in the Antarctic region, to take the place of that which had been exhausted in the north.

At the same time they readily fell in with the suggestion that the voyage should have also a scientific interest. The vessels were accordingly equipped with the necessary apparatus, and men who were qualified to engage in the work of scientific observation and research accompanied the ship.

The hopes of the owners were not justified, nor were the scientists successful, and the vessels had to be content with cargoes of seal skin instead of whalebone ; but others thought they might succeed where these had failed, and a German expedition on the same lines followed. The Germans, however, although they made some interesting discoveries and did some useful work as explorers, found, as all others must find, that commerce and science cannot be successfully combined in work of this kind.

Next a Norwegian entered the field—Svend Foyn, of Töusberg, a notable whale fisher. He was at the time a veteran of eighty-four, and too old, therefore, to engage in active work ; but he was keenly interested in the enterprise of his countryman, Mr. H. J. Bull, who was trying to organize an expedition to the South Pole. He placed a whaling ship at Mr. Bull's disposal ; and under command of Captain Leonard Kristensen, with Mr. Bull on board, the vessel, christened the *Antarctic*, sailed for the south in September, 1893. The results of the voyage were disappointing ; but they had their share in maintaining interest in the Antarctic and in helping to keep alive that enthusiasm for the work of exploration which had unaccountably fallen to such a low ebb.

An account of the voyage of the *Antarctic* was read at a Geographical Congress in London in 1895 ; and the Congress passed a resolution in the course of which it was stated that " the exploration of the Antarctic regions is the greatest piece of geographical work still to be undertaken."

Following this came two expeditions, one under the Belgian and one under the British flag, but both were in Norwegian built vessels, and both were manned principally by Scandinavian sailors. These accomplished a certain amount of successful scientific work, but neither they nor a subsequent expedition under the auspices of the German Government did anything more than Ross had accomplished half a century earlier towards the actual solution of the problem of the South Pole.

It cannot be doubted, however, now that the South Pole has actually been reached, that the twentieth century will witness the final and complete conquest of the regions of the Antarctic. Ere the century was a year old a determined effort was made when Commander R. F. Scott, R.N., set sail in the *Discovery* for the South Pole ; or rather, according to the official statement of the main object of the expedition—" to determine as far as possible the nature and extent of that portion of the South Polar lands which the ship should be able to reach ; and to conduct a magnetic survey."

Captain Scott wintered five hundred miles farther south than anyone had ever ventured before ; and when winter gave place to spring he organized sledge journeys. More than one of these was accomplished under circumstances of extreme difficulty and danger, but the brave explorers never wavered in their determination to overcome every obstacle, and the result of their toils and trials was a splendid addition to the world's knowledge of the geography of the far south ; and through their efforts the probability of reaching the South Pole was considerably increased.

During this voyage the *Discovery* spent in all two years and two months within the Antarctic Circle, and arrived home in September, 1904. Her commander's greatest triumph was that he was able to show that there was good reason to believe that the great Southern Barrier is the edge of an immense field of ice, which in some remote period filled the Antarctic sea, but which is now so far reduced in thickness as to be afloat with the sea running under it for hundreds of miles.

Voyaging along this barrier, Captain Scott came to King Edward's Land, and discovered subsequently that the volcanos Erebus and Terror stand, not on continental land, but on an island. More important still, he located the true position of the South Magnetic Pole in Victoria Land.

It has to be borne in mind that, as already stated, it was never the purpose of Captain Scott's expedition to reach the South Pole. Yet he did, in point of fact, approach within 463 miles of that ultimate goal—an achievement far beyond the attainment of any previous explorer, although it was surpassed in 1909 by Shackleton, whose daring

CAPTAIN AMUNSDEN AT THE SOUTH POLE.

advance brought him within ninety-seven geographical miles of the Pole.

In 1911 Captain Scott again set out in the *Discovery* for the Antarctic ; and again he stated plainly that his mission was not so much a "dash to the South Pole " and a speedy return to civilization, as an extended investigation of the seas and lands surrounding that point.

There can, of course, be no doubt that had it been compatible with the avowed purpose of his voyage, Captain Scott would have made an effort to get to the Pole ; but he has been out-distanced in the race towards that objective by a brave and daring Norwegian, Captain Amundsen, who, according to his own narrative, reached the South Pole on December 14th to 17th, 1911.

The Norwegian has achieved a remarkable triumph, and none will grudge him the full honour that is his due ; but still it remains true—and Captain Amundsen will be the first to acknowledge the fact—that the way to the South Pole was paved by the earlier enterprise of Captain Scott, to whom all praise must be given for his pioneer work during the ten years preceding the ultimate triumph of the brave Norwegian.

It is more than strange that within two years of the attainment of the North Pole, the South Pole also should have been reached ; but it by no means follows that with the achievement of these splendid triumphs the work of the explorer in latitudes farthest north and south is at an end. Much remains of exploration and discovery to be accomplished; and it may be taken for granted that although the goals for centuries so dear to the hearts of Britain's bravest sons have at last been won by heroes of other nations, yet the best of British brain and nerve is still available, and will be cheerfully sacrificed, if need be, in the pursuit of further and fuller knowledge of those " ends of the earth " which have had in the past and will continue to have in time to come an irresistible attraction for the most courageous men of our race.

HEADLEY BROTHERS BISHOPSGATE, E.C.; AND ASHFORD, KENT.

ND - #0085 - 220323 - C0 - 229/152/18 - PB - 9780282508364 - Gloss Lamination